only in your dreams

^a gossip girl_{novel}

Gossip Girl novels by Cecily von Ziegesar:

only in your dreams
a gossip girl novel

by
Cecily von Ziegesar

LITTLE, BROWN AND COMPANY
New York ∾ Boston ∾ London

Little, Brown and Company
Time Warner Book Group
1271 Avenue of the Americas, New York, NY 10020
Visit our Web site at www.lb-teens.com

First Edition: 2006

ALLOYENTERTAINMENT   Produced by Alloy Entertainment
151 West 26th Street, New York, NY 10001

ON THE COVER: dresses—**ABS Evening**,
sweater—**H&M**, sweater—**Bibelot @ Susan Greenstadt**,
earrings—**Yvette Fry Inc.**, **Chanel** charm bracelet—stylist's own

ISBN: 0-316-01182-7

10 9 8 7 6 5 4 3 2 1
CWO
Printed in the United States of America

She is pure Alice in Wonderland, and her appearance and demeanor are a nicely judged mix of the Red Queen and a Flamingo.

—Truman Capote

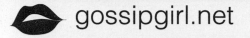
hey people!

It's been summer for about five minutes and already the city sidewalks are a hundred degrees. Thank God we can finally ditch our tired, hideous blue-and-white seersucker school uniforms— for *good*. Unless we decide to resurrect them for our first college Halloween party. Pleated kilts drive boys wild!

It was hard work surviving four years of high school, balancing partying, shopping, studying, partying, and shopping with just the right amount of grace and poise to land us in the Ivy League. We did it, though, and we've got the diplomas—and the graduation presents (*vroom, vroom, vroom!*)—to prove it.

In case you've had your head under a rock all year long, we're the kids who play as hard as we shop, and now that we've amassed our new summer wardrobes, it's time to get down to some serious play. You know us, and it's okay to admit it: you wish you were one of us. We're the girls strolling around Manhattan in crisp Marni sundresses and who-cares-if-we-ruin-them Jimmy Choo flip-flops. We're the tanned-since-spring-break-in-St.-Barts boys on the rooftop of the Met slugging Tanqueray and tonic from antique silver flasks. Summer's here, and those tedious worries like APs and SATs are over. The next couple of months are all about the good stuff: love, sex, fame, and *infamy*. Speaking of which . . .

**the most famous girl in town is about to become
even more famous**

She's a local legend already, but could she be headed for a whole new level of notoriety? Like, *Vanity Fair* covers and red-carpet premieres? It sure looks that way now that **S** has managed to land the only summer job worth *getting*: a starring role in a major Hollywood movie headed up by potentially insane rogue director Ken Mogul, playing opposite that gorgeous, golden-stubbled megastar **T**. *Swoon*. Judging from her history, **T** will soon be her leading man offscreen, too. Some girls really do have all the luck.

Even though everyone thought **B** was *destined* for the part, she appears to have gotten over losing out to her best friend . . . again. Maybe she's getting used to it, or maybe she's too busy cavorting with her delicious-looking new boyfriend between the perfectly pressed 600-thread-count cream-colored Egyptian cotton Claridge's of London hotel sheets to care. That's right: her whirlwind affair with that strapping English gentleman Lord **M** has changed settings from steamy New York to swanky London, and I can only imagine they're putting **B**'s hotel suite to good use. Of course, Lord **M**'s manor is purported to be even nicer than Claridge's, if that's possible—so why isn't she staying with him there? We'll find out soon enough: word of her escapades is already making its way back across the pond.

Scandalous information about our favorite perpetually stoned but still perpetually cute **N** is also making its way back to the city— although he's only a jitney ride away, in the summer-lovin' Hamptons. He's doing hard time on Long Island after that pesky stealing-Viagra-from-his-lacrosse-coach-and-almost-not-graduating episode. I hear he's already tan and persistently sweaty from all the reroofing he's doing at his coach's house. Some of the local ladies have been doing drive-bys just to get a peek at him with his shirt off. Meanwhile, on *this* side of Long Island—that's Brooklyn, FYI—**V** was seen enjoying the spoils of her short live-in with **B**. Hello, black silk DVF wrap dress! Only **B** would leave *that* behind like a used toothbrush. No one knows if **V** was having a fling with both sides of that stepsibling duo or not, but both **A** and **B** have moved on. Literally. Last I heard, **A** had taken up with a tattooed belly dancer in Austin, Texas, with two boxer puppies of her own. Thank goodness for **D**—he's been seen all over town frantically checking out the city like a tourist. Looks like someone's getting sentimental about his big move out west this fall.

Your e-mail

 Dear GG,

So there I was, in Heathrow Airport on my way to this totally fruity British boarding school my parents are making me start this summer, when whom should I see but **B**, aka the girl of my dreams. I thought my problems were solved, until I arrived on campus and heard three *very* disturbing rumors:

1) **B** is not only dating some English douche bag, she's *engaged* to him.

2) *He's* already engaged to someone else.

And, craziest of all:

3) Lord Douchebaggio isn't satisfying **B**'s womanly needs, if you catch my drift. Maybe he's too tired out from spending time with his fiancée?

Help a brother out, here. I'm going to freak the F out if I don't find a girl who knows that soccer is *not* called football.
—B Back on the Market?

P.S. *I* can go all night.

 Dear BB on the M,

I don' t know how they do it in England, but here in America seventeen is *way* too young to get married. Hello, we haven't even hooked up with our freshman year hall mates yet! Sit tight. Nothing lasts forever. . . .
—GG

P.S. All night, huh? What did you say you look like?

Dear GG,

It took a lot of begging and pleading, but I finally convinced my dad to shell out for a summer rental in Southampton just for me and my friends. Now we're here and no one else is. What gives?
—No Sex on the Beach

Dear NSOTB:
If you must know, getting to the Hamptons too early in the season is a little . . . well, tacky, unless you *have* to be there, like some people I know. In the meantime, why not shake it up? You've got a whole house at your disposal—fashion those palm-frond-patterned ABC Carpet & Home sheets into togas and get into the college spirit!
—GG

Sightings

B accusing a Virgin Atlantic bag handler of stealing one of her *many* Cosabella lace thongs from her Tumi duffel. That's what you get for flying commercial! **S** reading—*reading?* Hello, school's out!—a tattered paperback copy of *Breakfast at Tiffany's* on a shady bench in Central Park. No doubt she'll reminisce about it someday on *Inside the Actors Studio.* A sweaty **N** pumping up and down and up and—there goes my imagination!—through East Hampton center on his old red Schwinn ten-speed. What happened to the Range Rover? **V** at Bonita, that tiny, rustic Mexican place in Williamsburg, asking someone to wipe down the table before she sat down. Maybe **B** really did rub off on her. **D** cruising up and down West End Avenue for hours—where's he supposed to *park* that big blue Buick pimpmobile he scored as a graduation present, anyway?

That's all for now. I'm out of here. After all, you don't have to be an MIT-bound math geek to realize there are only eleven weeks of summer—a mere seventy-seven days—before we have to grapple with things like coed dorms and declaring a major in fashion design and maybe a torrid extracurricular affair with that probably-pretty-cute-under-his-tweed-blazer-and-bow-tie English lit professor. But let's not get ahead of ourselves: it's hot outside, and things are already getting steamy. Life is full of mystery—not to mention cute girls in polka-dot bikinis and hot guys in pastel-colored surf shorts. The summer, with its lack of rules and schedules, provides the perfect setting for some severe misbehavior. Right now, I'm taking my new oversized pale pink Gucci sunglasses, a copy of French *Elle*, some Guerlain SPF 45 sunblock, and a cozy turquoise-and-tangerine-striped Missoni towel and hitting the park. Which part of the park? Wouldn't you like to know?

You know you love me.

gossip girl

the honeymooners

"Good morning, madam!" trilled a female voice in a super-perky British accent.

Blair Waldorf sighed and turned over onto her side. She'd been in London three days but still wasn't over her jet lag. She didn't mind, though: it was a small price to pay to see her movie-star-handsome, real-life-English-blueblood boyfriend, Lord Marcus.

Wendy, one of the three maids whose round-the-clock services came with Blair's penthouse suite at Claridge's, clacked across the blond parquet floors and deposited a heavy mahogany tray onto the king-size bed, which was so big Blair had divided it up into four sections: one for sleeping, one for eating, one for watching TV, and one for sex. So far, *that* section had remained unused. Wendy drew the thick maroon velvet curtains on the massive wall of windows, flooding the enormous room with light. It reflected off the opulent gold-filigree ceiling and bounced off the gilded mirrors that lined the attached dressing room.

"Ouch!" Blair cried, pulling one of the six sumptuous goose-down pillows over her head to shield her eyes from the sun.

"Breakfast as requested, Miss Waldorf," announced Wendy, lifting the silver cover off the tray to reveal a barfy-looking mush of watery scrambled eggs, massive greasy sausages, and a pool of stewed tomatoes.

Classic English cuisine. Yum.

Blair smoothed her tousled chestnut hair and straightened the straps of the soft pink Hanro cami she'd worn to bed. The food looked disgusting but smelled delicious. Oh well, she deserved a little treat, didn't she? She'd worked up an appetite the day before, walking around West London sightseeing.

If you call Harrods, Harvey Nichols, and Whistles *sights*.

"And your paper," added Wendy setting the *International Herald Tribune* on the tray with a flourish. Blair had requested the daily paper when she checked in—a Yale woman had to keep up on world events, after all. So what if she hadn't exactly gotten around to the reading part?

"Will that be all?" Wendy asked primly.

Blair nodded and the maid disappeared into the sitting room. Blair speared one of the huge sausages with her fork and picked up the paper, skimming the front page. But the tiny typeface and matter-of-fact photographs were so boring she couldn't concentrate. The only paper she ever read was the Sunday Styles section of the *New York Times*, if only to scan the charity event pictures for familiar faces. Why would a worldly woman like herself need to read world news, anyway? She *was* world news.

Blair had always been impulsive, but her presence in London had actually been Marcus's idea. His graduation present to her—other than the ridiculously extravagant Bvlgari earrings—had been a plane ticket to London. Blair had envisioned rainy weeks locked in his enormous stone castle having chain-sex—the equivalent of chain-smoking—stopping only to gnaw on a cold leg of mutton or whatever medieval snack was stored in the castle's primitive but well-stocked kitchen. But Marcus had been so busy working for his dad all he ever had time for was lunch and a brief snog.

Dropping the unopened paper onto the floor, she scanned her bedside table for British *Vogue*—she'd stocked up on all the English magazines so she'd know what to buy and where to buy it—when her new razor-thin Vertu phone chimed prettily. There was only one person who had her new London telephone number.

"Hello?" she answered as sexily as she could with a mouth full of scrambled egg.

"Darling," Lord Marcus Beaton-Rhodes greeted her in his charming British accent. "I'm coming round. Just wanted to make sure you were up, love."

"I'm up, I'm up!" Blair was unable to control her excitement. She'd spent the last two nights alone, and her horniness was bubbling over into near-frenzy. How they'd made it this far without actually doing it, she wasn't sure. Was this their chance for a morning interlude sans knickers?

"Right," he continued in his charmingly straightforward way. "I'll be by shortly. And I've got a surprise."

A surprise! thought Blair giddily as she shut her phone. That was *just* the kind of wake-up call she needed to get her out of bed. She scurried to the bathroom, discarding clothes as she went. Could it be roses and caviar? Chilled champagne and oysters? It was kind of early in the morning for that, but judging from the last present he'd given her—the Bvlgari pearl earrings, with their dangling gold *B*s—it was bound to be good. Some equally exquisite symbol of his undying love? Everyone back in New York was so insanely jealous of her perfect English boyfriend that they'd spread rumors Marcus was already engaged. There was only one way to put *that* rumor to rest forever: return to New York wearing his ring. Preferably a flawless, four-carat, emerald-cut diamond, although an old family heirloom would do.

How humble of her.

Lord Marcus had initially invited her to spend the summer at his father's Knightsbridge mansion, but when he'd picked her up from Heathrow in his chauffeur-driven cream-colored Bentley he'd taken her straight to Claridge's. "We simply haven't got the room, sweetheart," Marcus whispered directly into her ear, his hot breath sending shivers down her spine as the desk attendant handed her the room key. "Plus, when I come over, we'll have complete privacy."

Well, that's hard to argue with.

Blair wasn't sure what Marcus's dad did for a living, but it had something to do with bonds, and whatever it was sounded very boring. Marcus was interning at his dad's office for the summer, and late nights and early mornings meant he had hardly any energy for . . . sex. Blair had only done it a few times with Nate Archibald, and she was beyond eager to try it with someone older and more experienced, like Marcus—not that sex with Nate had been so bad.

Her rosemary La Mer bath tonic and minty Marvis toothpaste masking the stink of scrambled egg and tomato, she hurried back to the bedroom and hopped into bed, wearing only a light sheen of lavender-scented bath water, Chanel No. 5 perfume, and the Bvlgari earrings she hadn't taken off once since her graduation party at the Yale Club a little over two weeks ago.

After ditching Vanessa Abrams's small apartment in dingy and weird Williamsburg, with no intention of moving back to the crazy world she used to call home, Blair had decided to live at the Yale Club. She and Lord Marcus had met in the elevator, and his hot accent and neatly ironed jeans had gotten to her right away. Fate had it that their rooms were side by side, and she could imagine the feel of his sexy English breath on her neck even before they'd kissed—which had happened that very night. After pouring her heart out to him over six or seven cosmos, Blair was so sure she'd found the love of her life, she practically threw herself at him. She was too tipsy—and he was too much of a gentleman—to do more than kiss. But all *that* was about to change.

Blair draped the sheets over her body and lit a cigarette, striking a pose that said, *I'm on my honeymoon and worn out from doing it, but what the hell, let's do it again.* She grabbed the newspaper off of the floor and propped up the front page so it looked like she was reading it. There. Perfect. An intellectual sexpot. A worldly woman who read all about international crises—and preferred to discuss said crises *in bed*. If only she had a pair of vintage fifties reading glasses to perch on the tip of her nose.

All the better to see you naked with!

As if on cue, Lord Marcus flung the bedroom door open and Blair turned her head slowly, as if she could barely stand to break away from the current poultry deficit in Asia. He was wearing a perfectly tailored charcoal summer suit with an olive James Perse T-shirt underneath that made his striking green eyes look serious and deep and oh-so-promising.

"What's this, then?" he asked, furrowing his golden-brown eyebrows. "Remember I said I had a surprise?"

"I've got a surprise for you too," Blair cooed sexily. "Come look under the sheets."

"Right," he continued a little impatiently. "Well, put on your clothes, love."

"I don't want to," Blair complained, pouting.

He hurried across the room and kissed her quickly on the nose. "Later," he promised. "Now throw on some clothes and meet me downstairs in the lobby." Then he turned and left the room, leaving her perfumed, well-moisturized, and depilated body naked and alone.

This better be a good surprise.

Blair emerged from the wood-paneled elevator in a hastily chosen ensemble: a chocolate brown Tory Burch tunic (thank you, Harrods), a favorite pair of old True Religion jeans, and clunky gold Marc by Marc Jacobs clogs. She looked like a jet-setter on holiday. Just right for a weekend jaunt to Tunis in Lord Marcus's private jet. Could *that* be the surprise?

The grand, chandelier-lit marble hotel lobby was abuzz with activity, but Blair noticed a hush fall over the crowd as she crossed the tiled floor, her clogs clopping noisily, to the overstuffed black velvet chaise where Marcus sat waiting for her. He was so goddamn handsome Blair couldn't help admiring him, like he was a painting or some rare piece of sculpture, and it was hard to resist plunging her fingers into the thick waves of his golden-brown hair. She was so busy mentally rhapsodizing over her gorgeous English lover that she barely noticed he was holding hands with someone who was *definitely* not her.

Ding, ding. Hello?

Forgetting the romantic jaunt to Africa, Blair's eyes narrowed at the horsy blonde holding her boyfriend's hand. *What the fuck?*

"Blair, at last," Lord Marcus greeted her smoothly, standing but not letting go of his companion's hand. "This, my dear, is my darling cousin Camilla, the one I told you about. My soul mate. She's in town for a couple of weeks. We were practically twins growing up! Isn't that the most marvelous surprise?"

"Marvelous," echoed Blair, throwing herself onto a nearby armchair. She didn't remember hearing anything about any cousin Camilla.

But then, listening had never been her strong suit.

"I'm so delighted to meet you," said Camilla, staring down her long, prominent nose—the kind of schnozz even the best plastic surgeon couldn't fix. Her pale English complexion was layered with comical amounts of beige powder and primary-red blush. Her legs were clownishly long and skinny, like she'd been stretched on one of those old-fashioned lengthening machines Blair had tried to find on eBay.

"Mimi just turned up yesterday morning, unannounced," Lord Marcus explained. "Imagine, like a lost waif, with bags in hand." He chuckled.

"Yes, well, thankfully I can count on my dear Mar-mar to open up his home to me," Camilla gushed, casually running her free hand through her long, flaxen hair. Hair that could easily be cut off in the middle of the night.

Wait—his *home*?

"You're staying at his place?" demanded Blair rudely, already hating the crooked-toothed Camilla and her ugly yellow Indian silk sundress, which probably cost thousands but looked like a tablecloth. "But I thought there wasn't room."

"There's always room for *family*," Lord Marcus answered, squeezing Camilla's talonlike hand before turning back to Blair. "Not to worry, sweetheart. We'll all have a grand time together."

Sure they will.

one is the loneliest number

"Archibald!" Coach Michaels yelled up at the roof. "I want to hear your lazy ass banging those shingles. Now!"

"Yes, sir," Nate Archibald muttered as he watched Coach climb into his blue minivan and back out of the short driveway, honking a cheerful *beep beep be-beep* as he sped off down the suburban Hampton Bays street. Nate could picture him popping Viagra and jacking off to the pornos he probably kept in the glove compartment.

Douche bag, Nate added silently. Sweat stinging his eyes, he ran a hand across his forehead and frowned down at the black-shingled roof. *Idiot,* he told himself for the hundredth time that morning. It was only nine o'clock, but the brutal sun was pounding down, the scratchy shingles were tearing up his knees, and his back throbbed. Nate straightened up to full height and pulled off his drenched lime-green Stussy T-shirt. Then he dropped his hammer and sat down, even though the roof was so hot he could feel it burning his ass through his shorts.

He dug around in his pockets for the lovingly hand-rolled Thai stick joint he'd been smart enough to stash there the night before. Nate pulled out the yellow plastic lighter he kept tucked into his sock and lit the joint, inhaling deeply.

Wake and bake. The breakfast of champions.

His fuckup was costing him, that was for sure, but Nate

was determined not to let one mistake ruin his whole summer. His days belonged to Coach Michaels, but his nights were still his, and he had his parents' place on Georgica Pond all to himself, since his folks preferred the splendid isolation of their compound up in Mt. Desert Island, Maine.

Nate flipped open his cell and scrolled through his contact list until he got to the first person he knew with a house in the Hamptons. There was no sense letting the perfect party house go to waste.

Waste not, want not.

"Hey, it's Charlie," said the voicemail recording. "I'm out of the country for a couple of weeks, but leave me a message and I'll check you when I get back. Later."

Damn. Nate hung up without leaving a message.

He scrolled some more until he came to the number for Jeremy Scott Tompkinson, another friend from school. Nate half remembered hearing something about how Jeremy was spending the summer out in LA, taking acting classes or something lame like that.

The only guy Nate knew for sure was in the Hamptons was Anthony Avuldsen, so Nate tried him too, but he didn't answer his phone either. He was probably still sleeping; no one with any sense would be awake this early in the morning.

Frowning, Nate took another deep drag on his joint. He could just imagine the endless march of hot, sweaty days and lonely, quiet nights before he would finally pack up and head off to Yale in the fall.

Poor baby.

From his perch on the roof, Nate could see the coach's wide backyard, the very yard he'd be in charge of mowing and landscaping for the next few weeks. He'd been so preoccupied, he hadn't noticed the best part of the view: the coach's wife, lying poolside, sunning herself in the bright morning rays, topless. She was a mom and she wasn't young, but she wasn't that old, either. At least her boobs had aged well. He'd seen

The Graduate, and he'd never been with an older woman. Shit could happen. Maybe working for the coach without pay wouldn't be so bad after all.

Or maybe the sun is getting to him.

v's date with destiny

Teetering ever so slightly on her black peep-toe Celine platform sandals—okay, so they were technically Blair's, but she knew her onetime roommate would never come back to Williamsburg to collect any of the stuff she'd left behind—Vanessa thwacked over the cobblestones of the too-trendy-for-a-place-that-smells-like-dead-meat Meatpacking District toward the unmarked rusty door of Ken Mogul's massive live/work loft.

Despite her classmate Serena van der Woodsen's drunken promises to put a good word in with him at Blair's wild graduation party a couple of weeks before, Vanessa Abrams had never seriously expected to hear from Ken Mogul again. Earlier that year, he'd taken an interest in her career when some nearly-X-rated film footage she'd shot of Jenny Humphrey and Nate Archibald hooking up in Central Park surfaced online and tried to take her under his wing as a protégé. But Vanessa didn't like the idea of being under *anyone's* wing, and working on a major Hollywood production out in LA wasn't exactly her thing. She was more a dead-pigeons-and-used-condom film auteur than maker of big teen blockbusters, but *Breakfast at Fred's* was going to be shot right on her doorstep at Barneys uptown. It was tempting to write it off as a learning experience. Still, something about it made her uneasy.

She rang the buzzer marked only with the director's initials and waited, fiddling nervously with her clothes. Nearly her entire outfit had been garnered from the spoils Blair had left behind. She'd paired a black sleeveless Mayle cowl-neck top with her own tattered black jeans, Blair's clunky Celine sandals, and the steel-gray leather DKNY messenger bag Blair used to carry her laptop in. The look was sophisticated and artsy: she looked like someone who didn't care about things like looking sophisticated.

Like she *ever* cared?

Suddenly the door flew open to reveal an incredibly tall girl sporting super-short cutoffs and a pink tank-top. Her skin was dark brown and flawless; her hair was long, jet black, and perfectly straight; and her eyes were huge, green, and sparkling. She smiled, showing off a mouthful of absolutely perfect white teeth.

All the better to eat you with . . .

"Yeah?" the Afro-Asian model-goddess demanded with a hostile grimace. She looked almost like an evil character in that Xbox game Jade Empire, and Vanessa could imagine being decapitated with a flick of her long, lean, fighting-machine wrist.

"Um, yeah, I'm here to see Ken."

"Come on up," Jade Empire muttered, turning around. The heavy steel door slammed shut as Vanessa followed her up a narrow cement staircase and into a huge, bright, open room. A forest of rusting steel columns supported the vaulted ceiling, and a bank of windows showcased an incredible view of the Hudson River. The vast space was divided by a long, open bookcase and was overflowing with heavy art books and vinyl records, framed photographs and dusty vases. The latest Arcade Fire album blasted from tiny Bose speakers mounted to the top of the bookcase, and the music echoed all around.

"He's in here somewhere," Jade Empire explained, clearly disinterested. "You've got an appointment, right?"

"I think so."

"Well, just hang out. He'll show up sooner or later. Good luck with whatever it is." She shrugged and kicked off her beaded yellow Chinese slippers and shuffled away into the depths of the loft, disappearing behind the bookcase.

Vanessa turned to the wall behind her, which was covered from floor to ceiling with framed photographs of all different sizes. She recognized some of them—they were Ken Mogul's own work. Before meeting him, Vanessa had worshipped the filmmaker, and she knew everything he'd ever done. His favorite place in the world was Capri, in Italy, and before turning to filmmaking, Mogul had been a renowned photographer. Mixed in with his art photos of half-nude models lolling around on litter-strewn subway platforms were snapshots of Ken crammed into nightclub booths beside famous faces like Madonna, Angelina Jolie and Brad Pitt, and David Bowie.

"Like what you see?" came a gravelly voice from behind her.

Vanessa turned to see the taut, stubbly face of Ken Mogul himself. He had the unnerving habit of seeming not to blink, and he fixed his slightly bloodshot bulging blue eyes on her with a crazed smile. He wore a plaid flannel vest and old Levi's chopped off at the knees.

"Here's the deal." He went on without waiting for her response. He wheeled around and Vanessa had no choice but to follow him past the massive bookshelf and into an enormous office with a garage-door-size window. "Here. Sit." He poured Vanessa a tall glass of what looked like chilled mint tea from a green glass pitcher and pointed to a red leather Eames chair across from a paper-strewn midcentury modern table. He poured a glass for himself and sank down into a desk chair, swiveling it aimlessly before tilting back and resting his feet on the desk. "It's a money job, is all, but just between us, *Breakfast at Fred's* is going to fucking rule. Don't tell the producers, but this is not your average teen flick. I'm thinking Godard. Something human, humorous, and freaking *dark*."

"Uh-huh," murmured Vanessa, sipping her tea. Not only was she distracted by the director's office artwork—over his desk hung a bigger-than-life-size picture of the director himself, completely naked, splashing in the waves with the bitchy Jade Empire skank—but she hated this kind of pretentious art talk.

Better get used to it, Miss NYU Film School.

"So, what do you say?" asked Ken, openly picking his nose and flicking the findings onto the floor. "I know it's a major studio, I know it's big budget, I know it's romantic comedy. But those are all the reasons I need you. I need your vision to help me deliver something that's going to make the movie-going public sit up and take notice. "

As if they hadn't already.

Vanessa stared out the window at some elevated train tracks that had been abandoned decades before and were now sprouting trees and grass, and a big building under construction on the next block. It was everything she was against: a major studio's romantic comedy for teenagers. But Ken Mogul *needed* her; how many incoming NYU freshmen could say the same thing? Plus, it sounded like a shitload of fun, and she had fuck-all to do that summer. That was why she'd come there today in the first place: sheer boredom.

She turned back to Ken. "I'll have to think about it."

Ken took his feet off the desk and fiddled with his papers, finally unearthing a beaten pack of cigarettes. He stuck one in his mouth but didn't light it. "The female lead was supposed to be my wife," Ken continued, "but, as you already know, I've decided to go in another direction."

"Wife?" Vanessa could hardly believe that anyone would dream of marrying a googly-eyed, neurotic, conceited freak like Ken Mogul.

"Heather. I think she showed you in."

Miss Congeniality was Mrs. Mogul?

"Oh, right." Vanessa couldn't resist taking another peek at

the nudie photo behind the desk. It looked like a scene from a pirated porn movie.

Freaks of the Caribbean?

"Well, now she's not speaking to me because I've decided to go with Serena. Serena's going to be huge. And so are you."

"I'm honored," Vanessa replied. "I really am. But you'll have to let me think about it, okay?"

Better think fast, honey. Hollywood waits for no one!

s moves out

"I'm going to 169 East Seventy-first Street," Serena van der Woodsen said to the cabbie as she slid into the taxi's black vinyl backseat. She rolled down the window and let the warm late morning air blow across her face. Aah, summer. All her life summer had meant parties at her family's estate in Ridgefield, Connecticut, or long, sunny afternoons in the park, reading old *W* magazines and slurping Stoli-and-cranberry popsicles with Blair. Now, for the first time ever, Serena had a job. She turned a thick manila envelope over in her hands and removed the letter she'd already read several times:

Holly: You must suffer for your art. You must BE your part. Pack your bags. The keys in this envelope are the keys to your new life— the original life of Holly. See you soon. Kenneth.

It was an odd letter, sure, but what else did she expect from a world-famous eccentric like Ken*neth* Mogul? He was her director, so she figured she better do as directed.

She patted the two old monogrammed red-and-white-striped Kate Spade tote bags beside her. They still smelled deliciously like the ocean and suntan lotion and contained a stash of Cosabella underwear, one of her brother Erik's old Brown T-shirts that she'd swiped the last time he'd been home, a flimsy Milly sundress, her most comfortable Michael Kors flip-flops, a Cynthia Vincent pink-and-black paisley print jersey dress, her trusty Seven jeans, a second pair of flip-flops, just in case, and a white embroidered Viktor & Rolf top. Only the essentials.

She stared out the window at the grand steps of the Metropolitan Museum of Art, the lush trees of Central Park, the grand apartment buildings on Seventy-second Street, the panoramic vista of Park Avenue, and then at the unfamiliar, ugly modern towers on Third Avenue. Ew.

"We're here, miss," the cabdriver announced, grinning at her in the rearview mirror with a mouthful of gold-capped teeth. One tooth even had the initial *Z* stenciled into it. *Maybe for* Zorro *or* Zeus? Serena wondered.

"Oh." She pulled out her burgundy Bottega Veneta wallet and thumbed through the cash. Then she climbed out of the taxi, balancing her packed-to-the-gills tote bags, and scanned the putty-colored town houses for the right number.

There was number 171, and there was number 167, but there were some unmarked buildings in between the two, and she couldn't figure out which was hers. She lugged her bags to the nearest stoop and sat down. Judging from some of the boxy, low buildings on the street, the place she was moving into wouldn't be *quite* on par with what she was accustomed to. She dug out a cigarette and lit it, stepping aside as a stream of foul-smelling gray smoke billowed out of a grate in the gutter.

Wake up, Dorothy: you're not on the Golden Mile anymore.

It was funny how everything could change so quickly— she'd gone from being Serena van der Woodsen, senior at Constance Billard and sometimes-model, to being Serena the working actress. It didn't seem so long ago that her biggest worries had been remembering where the Catherine Malandrino sample sale would be this month, or bickering with Blair in the VIP room at Marquee, or hooking up with Nate wherever he wanted—which, for a short while, had been everywhere and all the time.

It's a hard-knock life.

"You lost?"

Serena looked up . . . and up, and up. Standing above her was a gorgeously tall guy with broad shoulders, preppily cut dark brown hair, a cleft in his wide chin, and pretty blue eyes. He was wearing a plain gray suit and stiff navy tie, but his smile was so charming she was willing to overlook his dorky office ensemble.

But would she be willing to overlook the dorky plaid boxers he was probably wearing underneath?

"I'm just looking for this address," Serena sighed, handing the stranger her keys with the number 169 painted on them in red.

Some girls really know how to work the damsel-in-distress thing.

"Well"—he grinned, "I think I know exactly where this building is. Because I actually kind of live there." He extended a hand to help Serena to her feet. "Hey, I'm Jason Bridges."

"Serena van der Woodsen," she replied, smoothing her Kelly green Lilly Pulitzer skirt, smiling the sort of sly, wide-eyed-ingenue smile that Audrey Hepburn was famous for.

No wonder she got the part.

Just like Holly Golightly, Serena was a master of the she-can't-possibly-be-that-beautiful-and-that-innocent-allure that made guys flock to her.

"Well, Serena." Jason bent down to pick up her two over-stuffed totes. "Let's head on home."

He unlocked the door to number 169, a white town house with black trim and ivy climbing up the side of it. He shoved the heavy old black door open to allow Serena to step inside first.

A true gentleman!

"So," he began as the door slammed behind him. "You visiting Therese?"

"No." Serena frowned as she inspected the vestibule's creaky wooden staircase, lit only by a pretty but dim wrought-iron chandelier. The whole place smacked of dead old lady, as though it hadn't been touched since its original owner died thirty years ago. Yet it was still charming and semi-grand, in its own way. "I'm moving in, I guess."

"You guess?" Jason laughed as he started to climb the wooden steps, which groaned and squeaked noisily. "What does that mean, exactly?"

"Well," Serena began, "I'm in this movie, and this morning I got a note from my director telling me to pack my bags and come here, and now here I am. I think it's to help me get into character or something."

"Movie star, huh?" Jason asked.

"Something like that," Serena answered, mildly embarrassed.

"Wow." He turned to shoot her a slow, shy smile. "This is a nice building, but I'd think most movie stars would just want to stay somewhere a bit more glamorous, like the Waldorf or something."

"We're doing a retelling of *Breakfast at Tiffany's*," she explained, choosing the exact words Ken Mogul had used to describe his big-budget debut, *Breakfast at Fred's*. "This is where Holly Golightly lived in the original movie, but I guess you probably knew that already. It's supposed to make me feel just like she does. It's my first movie."

"Oh yeah?" Jason asked as they reached the landing, where the black-and-white mosaic-tile floor was missing a few tiles. "What's it about?"

"It's about a wild city girl—that's my part—who meets this innocent guy from the country who's trying to make it as an actor." She conveniently left out that the guy would be played by super-hot actor Thaddeus Smith. "Then, this uptight Upper East Side girl wows him with her money . . . and things like lunch at Fred's, the restaurant at Barneys?" Serena hoped what she was saying made some sense. She had a tendency to ramble and lose track of the plot.

As if any guy she'd ever talked to even *cared*.

They turned up another staircase and Serena went on,

starting to feel a little winded as she spoke. "The other girl ruins his innocence, which is, like, the one quality that would make him a success as an actor—and turns him into a jaded New Yorker. Then it's up to my character to save him."

"So does that means we'll be neighbors all summer?" Jason asked, sounding adorably hopeful.

"Actually, just for a couple of weeks," she admitted. *Breakfast at Fred's* was a big-budget picture, but Ken Mogul had only twelve days scheduled for the actual filming.

They reached one landing and walked down a narrow hall. Then he turned and led her up another flight of steps.

"How far up are we going?" Serena wondered out loud. She was slightly out of breath.

Better lay off those hard-core French cigarettes.

They reached another landing, walked down another hallway, and started up another flight. Was it possible that he was just leading her up to some dark, hidden, date-rape lair? Should she be scared? She patted her skirt pocket, checking for her cell phone, just in case.

"I'm at my first job, too," he explained. "I'm a summer associate at Lowell, Bonderoff, Foster and Wallace. The law firm? I was there until four last night, so that's why I'm going to work now. I don't usually have to work so late, though."

At last they reached the top floor, where the ceiling was low and the hallway was dark. Serena could see the flush on Jason's cheeks. She wasn't sure if it was from all those damn stairs or if he was blushing because of her.

"Here we are," he announced.

She unlocked the door and pushed it open. Jason followed her inside and dropped her bags on the ground with a thud that echoed off the walls of the empty apartment. Two bare bulbs protruded from the urine-colored ceiling, which was marred with so many water stains, it almost looked like the orange-and-yellow tie-dye pattern had been painted on.

"It's nice," he observed gamely.

It *is?*

Serena strolled around the apartment's main room, almost losing her balance on the sloping, creaky wood floor. Three windows faced the street, with tattered screens and a view of the solid brick old people's home across the street. Out of the back window off the tiny kitchen, Serena recognized the fire escape from the original *Breakfast at Tiffany's,* where Holly Golightly had strummed her mandolin and sung "Moon River." Blair got teary every time they watched that scene. Serena pushed a window open. The apartment had a stale, claustrophobic, gag-inducing smell, like sweaty feet and sardines.

"But where's the furniture?" she asked, her voice dangerously close to a whine.

"And who's this?" Jason added. A black cat wandered into the living room from the bedroom at the back of the apartment.

Well, that explains the smell.

Serena pulled out her pack of Gauloises and poked her head out that famous kitchen window, hoping to feel inspired, but all she felt was nervous and a little lost. Why was she there again?

Because she was about to star in a major motion picture— *hello?*

"He's cute." In the kitchen, Jason crouched down to stroke the cat behind its ears.

Serena turned, lighting her cigarette as she watched her dark-haired, blue-eyed neighbor playing with the cat, who apparently lived in their building too.

See? The views aren't *all* bad.

d learns the art of customer service

"Excuse me, sir, can you tell me where I can find the romance novels?"

Daniel Humphrey was crouched on the floor, making sure the biographies were alphabetized by subject, not author. When working at the Strand, New York's best—and biggest—bookstore, it was important to pay attention to details like the proper arrangement of the biographies.

Whatever turns him on.

"We might have a few on the shelves by the stairs, but we don't have a romance section," Dan explained, unable to hide his displeasure.

"Thanks," the woman replied cheerfully as she strolled away to browse the dusty Johanna Lindsey books and whatever Nora Roberts novels were still left on the shelves.

The Strand was legendary not just for its incredible selection but also for its highly educated, highly snotty staff, and Dan was thrilled to have gotten the job. He'd seen the help-wanted poster after dropping his sister, Jenny, off at Kennedy on her impromptu trip to visit their mom in Prague and take some art classes, and he'd been feeling a little down about what he was supposed to do with his own summer. When he saw the poster in the store window, it really felt like a sign.

Now here he was, shelving books at the best store in town. But compared to other bookstores, the Strand had zero atmosphere. There was no music, no coffee. Just rows and rows of mismatched bookshelves crammed with books.

Pushing a creaky cart overloaded with dusty volumes, Dan made his way down the narrow aisle of the biography section. His job involved spending lots of time on his own and ignoring customers, which gave him plenty of time to think: about literature, about his poetry, about what Evergreen College in Washington state was going to be like, and mostly about what his last summer in New York—and his last summer with Vanessa—was going to be like. He'd made a big scene at his graduation when he'd declared he wouldn't be enrolling in college at all so he could stay by her side, but as it turned out, he was looking forward to driving out west in the rad metallic blue '77 Buick Skylark his dad had given him as a graduation present. It was the perfect car for a road trip; he'd be just like Jack Kerouac in *On the Road*, tearing up the highways and making love to the land and sky with the words that crept into his head as he drove along. He'd leave poems for all the women he met—the mysterious lover they'd never quite have. Until then, he'd have one last perfect summer in the city with Vanessa, his first love.

Dan grabbed a copy of Boswell's *Life of Johnson* off the top of his cart and crouched on the dusty wood floor of the store trying to find the spot where it belonged. His mind began to wander as the words came to him:

Hot hands steer the wheel
You're my gears, my pedals
Stir up the dust. Lust. Lust. Make it last

Sure, it was a little cheesy, but God, that was how he felt right now. He started making a mental list of classic romantic New York dates: Seeing Shakespeare in Central Park, riding the Staten Island Ferry just for the hell of it, watching the sun rise over the Fifty-ninth Street bridge just like Woody Allen and Diane Keaton in *Manhattan*. Maybe a drive out to Jones Beach in the Skylark, the salty wind blowing through the open windows, Vanessa's hair blowing behind them . . . Okay, well, not her hair—she basically had no hair—but maybe she could wear a long silk scarf or something. He could see it now. It was going to be the most romantic summer.

It's going to be *something*, that's for sure.

"Excuse me, do you have the Cliffs Notes for *Ulysses*?" a high-pitched male voice whispered barely audibly, interrupting Dan's reverie.

Cliffs Notes for James Joyce? The horror!

Dan scowled at the nerdy-looking goth kid who'd asked for his help. He was holding a Batman lunch box, and Dan realized he wasn't nerdy or goth so much as hopeless.

"Why don't you try reading the real thing?" he responded disparagingly.

Hopeless, who was actually probably older than Dan—an NYU student, maybe, or some poor asshole toughing it out in summer school so he could finally graduate at twenty-three—shrugged. "Boring."

Dan wanted to punch him in his skinny stomach, but he suddenly realized it was his job—no, his duty—to make this asshole read. He stood up. "Follow me."

He led the mindless goth kid into a small back room full of leather-bound classics and found a beautiful Everyman's Library copy of Joyce's masterpiece. Dan began to read aloud from a random page: "*Touch me. Soft eyes. Soft soft soft hand. I am lonely here. O, touch me soon, now. What is that word known to all men? I am quiet here alone. Sad too. Touch, touch me.*" Dan paused and looked up. "Come on, you know you want to," he urged.

The kid looked terrified, probably suspecting Dan was some sort of Strand-lurking literary pervert. He dropped his Batman lunch box and bolted.

Dan sat down on the floor to finish the page. He had to admit that James Joyce did always sort of turn him on.

Yes, it's going to be an interesting summer indeed.

helmets are almost as important as condoms

Nate stood up on the pedals of his vintage Schwinn, pushing them up and down with his feet, and then eased himself back onto the uncomfortable, unpadded leather seat. He liked to bike this way—pedaling as hard as he could and then sitting down to feel the warm summer breeze on his face. To the right, the waves rippled off the beach. On his left was a vineyard full of Chardonnay grapes. The air smelled like salt and gas-grilled steak. He listened to the satisfying crunch of the gravelly road under his wheels and grinned lazily.

His morning joint had done just the trick, and by the end of the day, he'd been kind of grooving on what was supposed to be his summer punishment. There was something soothing about physical labor. He'd spent the summer after tenth grade helping his dad build their sailboat, the *Charlotte*, up at his family's compound in Mt. Desert Isle, Maine, and the afternoon working on Coach Michaels's place kind of reminded him of that summer, although the setting—rows of houses and overpopulated beaches—wasn't quite as serene. Still, there was nothing like tough manual work, bright sunshine, and the reward of a cold Stella Artois when the day was done; and no distractions.

There were no classes to worry about: school was over at last, and Yale seemed impossibly far away. Blair, the girl he was pretty sure was the love of his life but who he could never seem to get it together for, was in England with her new aristocrat boyfriend, probably shopping, eating scones, and drinking way too much tea. Serena was back in the city becoming a movie star, and Jenny, the incredibly well-endowed freshman he'd somehow gotten involved with last winter, had been shipped off to Europe. He was better off far away from those three.

He grinned, realizing that this was how the whole summer would go: days of hard labor; bike rides back home; then a shower, a joint, and maybe some time by himself was just what he needed. Coach's house was in Hampton Bays, several miles from his own house in East Hampton, but it was like a different world, with its suburban houses and minivans and malls. It was just the kind of place that would help him refocus this summer, which was his plan. He didn't have his eye on any particular girl, and anyway, they tended to lead him into nothing but trouble. Maybe he was better off as a solo act.

As if he were ever alone for more than thirty seconds.

Nate had to climb off and push the squeaky bike up a particularly bad hill, wheezing from the effort. Sucking down three joints a day will do that to you.

Out of breath and sweating, he climbed back on the bike at the hill's summit and drifted down, letting gravity do the work. He looked down and poked at his forearm to see if the pink skin turned white when he touched it. It was something Blair used to do to him when they went to the beach together. After declaring him burned, she'd gently slather him with her fancy sunscreen. He pushed at his forearm again. Definitely a little cooked.

That's what you get for skipping the Coppertone!

Then he looked up and realized he was speeding straight for the road's shoulder. He pulled on the handlebars, swerving across the road, but he was going so fast that he wiped out. Hard.

There was a polite round of applause, like at a golf match.

Nate looked up, realizing he was splayed out in the dirt parking lot in front the Oyster Shack, a gray clapboard seafood joint about halfway between Coach's house and his family's hundred-year-old estate near Georgica Pond in East Hampton. A group of high-school-age kids was sitting at a picnic table, strewn with sweating beer bottles and baskets of fried food, and they were all staring at him.

"Shit," Nate muttered. Tiny pebbles were embedded in the palms of his hands, and he'd torn the faded lime-green Stussy shirt he'd been working in all day. He brushed the dirt from his hands and looked down at his cutoff khakis—no damage there.

Leave it to Nate Archibald to look even better covered with sweat, blood, and grime.

He crouched to examine the bike's front wheel. It was bent.

"Tough break."

Nate looked up. The voice belonged to a curvy, blue-eyed blonde who wore her curly dark blond hair pulled back tight and tucked under a red bandana. Her pink tube top was riding dangerously low and her denim miniskirt promisingly high. A lipstick-smeared straw poked out of the Coke she gripped in her left hand. She extended her right hand to Nate, her long, perfectly painted nails exactly the same shade of red as the can.

"Just ignore my friends," she told him apologetically.

Her skin was the same golden beige as that of every other girl who used the same shade of Clinique self-tanner, but beneath the beige was a smattering of freckles covering her nose, cheeks, shoulders, arms, and chest. Nate had learned from Blair that girls were usually more complicated than they first appeared, and this girl's prominent freckles seemed to suggest that she was more than just a typical Long Island babe.

Nate grinned as he took her hand and let her pull him to his feet. "Yeah, no problem," he answered sheepishly.

"You're going to need to get that looked at," Freckles advised, nodding at the bike.

"Yeah," muttered Nate. He wasn't that worried about the bike. The only thing that seemed worth looking at was right in front of him.

"I'm Tawny. I know a place where you can get your bike taken care of. But maybe I'll buy you an ice cream cone first."

Tawny? But isn't that the color of her self-tanner?!

"Sure." He'd smoked the roach from his morning joint before leaving Coach's place—hence the accident, maybe?—and ice cream sounded very appetizing indeed. "I'm Nate."

"So what's your story, Nate? I've never seen you around," Tawny asked as she skipped across the street to a tiny, faded blue house that was so small it looked like it was out of a cartoon. A couple of little kids were perched on the steps licking strawberry ice cream cones.

"Two vanilla cones," Tawny purred to the pimply guy behind the counter. She had the faintest hint of an accent, but Nate couldn't quite place it.

"No story." Nate idly kicked the side of the cartoon house with the toes of his battered Stan Smiths. He wanted to run his hands up and down her warm, freckled arms.

Tawny knelt down and smiled and laid a five-dollar bill on the counter, reaching inside the window to retrieve two pointy sugar cones piled high with creamy white scoops of ice cream. She handed one to Nate.

"Thanks." The ice cream started to melt immediately in the late afternoon sun, trickling down his hand. He licked it delicately.

Tawny touched his skinned knee gently. There was something about the way she did it—a possessiveness? A certainty? A particular *je ne sais quoi*—that reminded Nate of Blair. But this girl was nothing like Blair: Blair would never wear a pink tube top, or let an ice cream cone melt all over her hands, or . . . pay for food on a first date.

Date? That was fast.

"Are you okay?" Tawny asked, rising to her feet. She licked her pink, swollen-looking lips. "You look so serious."

The truth was, Nate was wondering what Tawny looked like without her tube top on. Was her chest freckled too? His hands itched just thinking about it.

"I'm just really glad I met you," Nate told her a little goofily. He dabbed his chin with a napkin. "We should hang out this summer."

A world record: Nate Archibald managed to swear off girls for three whole minutes.

love don't live here anymore

Vanessa slammed the rusty cab door and stared up at the weather-beaten brick façade of her Williamsburg apartment building, still mulling over Ken's job offer. She wished there was someone she could ask for advice, but she knew better than to call her self-absorbed, Vermont-living hippie parents. They'd just lecture her about art and commerce and "creative responsibility." She wished her sister Ruby was around—she was the only one Vanessa really trusted to talk to about these things.

A white Ford station wagon with a broken windshield was parked in front of the building where it had been for weeks. One of the back doors was missing, and the seats were piled with garbage bags and old blankets. Someone must have been living in it, which would explain the stench of urine that surrounded the car.

Nice.

Vanessa unlocked the building's complicated array of dead bolts and latches and clomped up the stairs, hesitating halfway up. There were voices coming from inside her apartment. Had she left the TV on? She tiptoed to the door and listened, not breathing. Yes, it was *definitely* voices, they were *definitely* coming from inside, and there was something very familiar about one of the voices.

Vanessa's older sister Ruby had been on a whirlwind tour

of Europe with her band, SugarDaddy, for eight weeks. An occasional postcard from Madrid or Oslo had appeared in the mailbox, and they'd spoken on the phone once, but the touring-rock-girl lifestyle wasn't all that conducive to staying in touch.

Vanessa threw the door open excitedly. "Ruby!" Vanessa cried, taking in her sister in her purple leather pants and her new matching shade of hair. It looked almost iridescent. "I can't believe you're back!"

"Hey," Ruby greeted her casually from the couch. She was straddling a skinny, stubbly-faced guy wearing black leather pants just like Ruby's purple ones. Ruby touched the tip of her cigarette to the tip of his to light it. She didn't get up to hug her sister, and her tone of voice was completely nonchalant, like Vanessa had just been at the grocery store to buy milk or something.

"Um, hi?" Vanessa was slightly taken aback. She closed the apartment door behind her.

"What's going on, sis?" asked Ruby, puffing on her Marlboro as she surveyed the apartment's Blairified decor. "I see you did some redecorating."

Vanessa didn't want to make small talk about Blair's renovations. Ruby was back just when she needed her most! "*Hello*, you're back! That's what's going on. How was the tour?"

Her older sister shrugged. "Berlin, London, Paris, Budapest. We rocked. It was incredible."

"All hail the conquering rock star. I'm Vanessa." She clomped over to the guy Ruby was straddling. He hadn't looked at her once.

"This is Piotr," Ruby explained, wiggling her purple-leather-clad ass as she said his name, as if just saying it was a real turn-on. "We met after our show in Prague."

"Hallo," Piotr replied in a stiff accent, exhaling a long plume of smoke as he spoke.

Charming.

"The apartment looks cool." Ruby sounded skeptical. She glanced around the room. "But how could you afford all this? The furniture, the drapes?"

"It's a long story," Vanessa answered, leaning against the lavender-painted wall and trying to look anywhere but at the fawn-colored suede couch where the filthy, scrawny Eastern European stranger was stretched out underneath her sister.

"Like the story of where you got those shoes?" Ruby asked, throwing her purple hair back. It was the same color as Willy Wonka's hat. "And that top? Jesus, look at you. You're a real fashion plate."

"I had a meeting." Vanessa felt hurt. Why was Ruby being such a bitch? If only the slimebag between her legs would get lost so they could order some sushi and have one of their sisterly heart-to-hearts.

"A word?" Ruby climbed down off of Piotr's lap. She nodded toward the kitchen.

Vanessa followed, wondering how long Ruby was going to be home. They leaned against the Formica countertop. "You two look pretty . . . serious," Vanessa observed.

"It's love," Ruby murmured wistfully, sounding surprisingly un-rocker chick. She did a little half-pirouette then stopped, pseudo-embarrassed, and leaned against the counter again.

"That's cool," Vanessa responded, irritated. It didn't look like they were going to be doing any sisterly bonding after all. She fiddled with the ceramic Statue of Liberty salt and pepper shakers Dan had given her in a fit of romantic corniness.

"Well, the apartment does look good, even if it's not what I expected to come home to," Ruby commented. "But I hate to think that you went to all this trouble when . . ."

"When what?" Vanessa asked suspiciously.

"Not to be the bearer of bad news, but . . . Piotr is going to be here for a while. Some local galleries are interested in him—he's a painter, did I mention? He does monolithic nudes with their canines. He's huge in the underground Prague scene, and he's hoping to break into Williamsburg."

Vanessa wasn't exactly sure what "monolithic nudes and their canines" meant, but she could imagine Ruby borrowing somebody's pit bull and posing for him butt-naked, teeth bared. "Good for him."

"Well, I kind of thought he'd stay here, with me," Ruby mumbled.

"That's kind of a tight fit," Vanessa muttered back. "But that's cool. We'll work it out."

"That's the thing," Ruby corrected her. "Piotr needs a studio. And since he can't afford to rent one, we were thinking . . . we'd turn the other room, your room, into his studio."

Ex-squeeze me?

"So, what, you're *kicking me out?*" Vanessa stopped fiddling and turned to face her sister. She'd been living with Ruby since she was fifteen. It was her home too.

"Well, this was always just a temporary solution. You know, like, while you were in high school. But now that you've graduated, it's time to strike out on your own, like I did when I was eighteen."

"Fine," Vanessa snapped. "That's cool. I get it, I'm all grown up and on my own now. I get it."

"Don't be like that," Ruby pleaded guiltily. "Come back and sit, let's talk things over a little more."

"No, it's cool, really. Let me just grab my stuff and I'll be out of Pita Bread or whatever-the-hell-his-name-is's hair immediately." Shaking a little, Vanessa stormed out of the kitchen and into the living room, where Pizza Face sat smoking some rotten-smelling Czech cigarettes. Vanessa snatched her still photograph of a dead pigeon off the wall above his head and tucked it under her arm. It was her favorite, and she wasn't about to leave it behind so he could copy it in one of his paintings. She could see it now: he'd become known as the "dead pigeon" artist, when all along it had been *her* dead pigeon and *her* freaking apartment.

A few minutes later, Vanessa crashed down the stairs, lugging her camera equipment and one giant black duffel bag. She burst out into the late afternoon sun and stumbled down Bedford Avenue, dodging indifferent, funkily dressed passersby and piles of dog shit and wondering where, exactly, she was going to go.

She dropped her duffel on the ground and sat, using the fully stuffed bag as a perch. Digging her cell phone from her pocket, she hit speed dial. There were two rings and then the familiar sound of Dan's voice.

"What's up?"

"My sister kicked me out." Her voice cracked. She tried desperately not to cry. "And I don't have any money, and I don't have anywhere to go, and I don't know what I'm going to do."

Guess she'll be taking that job.

s is for spirituality, among other things

"Hey," Dan whispered into his black Nokia cell as he ducked behind an aging metal bookshelf at the Strand. It was the kind of place only a guy who had read *Hamlet* five times could love. "I was just thinking about you."

He couldn't quite make out Vanessa's response: she sounded out of breath and near tears.

"Wait, wait," he soothed. He stacked up a pile of Ronald Reagan biographies and sat down on them. "Slow down. I didn't catch any of that."

"I said I've been kicked out of my apartment," Vanessa shouted. "Ruby's back from Europe and she has this new asshole Czech painter bullshit boyfriend and she told me to get lost."

"Shit," Dan muttered, looking around. He wasn't really supposed to be on his cell phone on the job.

"What am I going to do? Where am I supposed to go?"

"What about my place?" Dan asked, before he even had a chance to think about what he was saying. He fingered an old dusty hardcover about Walt Whitman and considered taking it home.

"Your place?" Vanessa repeated, pitifully. Dan wasn't sure he'd ever heard her sound so weak, and even though he kind of knew it was wrong, he sort of liked how it made him feel.

Like he was some macho stud and she was frail and helpless. He made a mental note to use the feeling for a poem.

Rice paper girl, I'm the quill, the ink, the well. . . .

"It'll be fine," he assured her. "Take your stuff, get on the subway, go to my place. The door's unlocked—you know my dad always leaves it open. I'll be home in a couple of hours."

"Really?" Vanessa asked tentatively. She'd always been so fiercely independent. Dan knew she hated asking for any favors. "Are you sure it's okay with your dad?"

"It'll be fine." He rubbed some dust off the top shelf and it sprinkled in his eye. "You'll see. I'll be there soon. Don't worry." He rubbed his eyes, listening to Vanessa breathe on the other end of the phone.

"On the plus side, Ken Mogul offered me a job today." Vanessa laughed bitterly. "It looks like I'm going to have to take it."

"That's awesome!" he cheered, though he couldn't help feeling a little disappointed. He was working, and now Vanessa was going to work too. That would definitely put a damper on his romantic plans. When would they have time to ride the tram to Roosevelt Island and drink sake in the park?

"Shit, that's my call waiting," she mumbled. Dan heard her take the phone from her ear. "It's Ken. I better get it. I'll see you at home, then? Your home, I mean."

"No," he corrected her. "Yours too."

Aw.

Dan pressed the end button on his cell and slipped back into the narrow aisle of the biography section. He smiled. Maybe Vanessa getting kicked out was actually the best thing that could happen to them. Living together would make their last summer before leaving for college so *intimate*. It would be even more memorable.

He grabbed a few of the Reagan biographies and crouched, trying to find a place for all of them on a shelf.

"Excuse me, I'm looking for a copy of *Siddhartha* and I just can't seem to find one. Can you help me?"

Dan rose from his crouching position, his knees cracking from bending over, ready with a clever barb about where to find enlightenment. But once he saw the customer, he swallowed his words.

She was about four inches taller than he was, with long wavy platinum blond hair pulled back in a no-nonsense ponytail. She wore a faded gray gym tee and white denim cutoffs and had matching green-and-white wristbands on both of her arms. She furrowed her brow a little, but even worried, her blue eyes twinkled. She looked like Marsha Brady, only sexier and dirtier looking, like Marsha Brady on her way home from her aerobic striptease class.

"Um, yeah," Dan finally replied, flustered. "Yeah, we should have a copy of *Siddhartha*. I'm sure we have one."

"Oh, good," Dirty Marsha cried, reaching out and squeezing his bony upper arm. "I really want to read it."

"Yeah," he muttered, leading her away from the presidential biographies and toward paperback fiction. "It's actually one of my favorite books."

It is?

"Oh, gosh, really?" Dan had never encountered a girl who managed to say "gosh" and not sound like a complete moron. "It comes so highly recommended by my yogi."

"Here it is," he announced, standing on his tiptoes and tugging on the book's thin blue spine. He handed it to her.

"Cool." She turned the book over to examine the back cover. "This looks really great. Thanks so much for your help. So you really liked it?" She gazed at him, her almond-shaped eyes matching the twilight blue of the book's faded cover.

"Well . . ." Dan paused. Books were his area of expertise— why couldn't he think of anything to say?

Maybe because he never read it?

"It was, um . . . inspiring."

"Great. I'm really looking forward to it." She cradled the book against her chest and leaned into Dan a bit more closely. "Maybe I'll come back when I've finished it and you can recommend another book for me?"

"I'm always happy to recommend books to our customers," he replied smoothly.

"Awesome!" she cried with cheerleaderish enthusiasm. "I'm Bree."

"Dan."

"Cool, Dan. This book isn't long, so I'll be back in a couple of days. Thanks again for your help!" She turned and strolled away, an actual bounce in her step. Dan watched her small, round butt, which closely resembled two scoops of French vanilla ice cream, disappear behind the News and Current Events section, before remembering that he'd just asked Vanessa to move in with him.

How, um . . . enlightened.

the family that plays together stays together

"Bravo!" cried Lord Marcus. "Darling, you're simply a natural at this!"

Camilla chuckled, tucking her long blond mane behind her ears as her red croquet ball rolled through the wicket and came to rest on a patch of perfectly manicured emerald green lawn in the back garden of the Beaton-Rhodes manor. It was the third match they'd played that day, and Camilla had won. Again.

"I learned from the master," she giggled excitedly.

"When is it going to be my turn?" Blair whined. She'd been waiting for ages to get her chance to swing the mallet. She was definitely in the mood to hit something.

Behind them the ivy-covered gray stone West London mansion rose up like a fortress. Blair hadn't been invited inside yet, nor had she met Marcus's parents.

"Mother has one of her headaches," he'd explained, causing Camilla to erupt into a fit of honking laughter. Blair wondered if Lady Rhodes had a tendency to bring a bottle of sloe gin to bed with her, but she didn't ask, preferring to glare menacingly at Camilla instead. There was something so "I'm *in* and you're *out*" about her, Blair just wanted to rip her head off like some kind of ugly royal cousin Barbie that would still be on the shelves at FAO Schwarz long after Christmas.

"I believe that ends our game," Lord Marcus called apologetically. "Shall we have another go?"

"Whatever," muttered Blair, sipping her fourth Bombay Sapphire martini of the afternoon. The sprawling ancient stone mansion was framed by hundreds of perfectly conical bushes. Even the massive trees had been trimmed into unnatural shapes. Blair was beginning to feel like Alice at the Queen of Hearts' palace in Wonderland. She lit a Silk Cut and puffed on it greedily. "Can we get some more refreshments?" she asked of no one in particular.

When in doubt, have another.

"I'm knackered," sighed Camilla as she collapsed into the wrought-iron chair next to Blair's. "Having fun?" she asked, putting her hand on Blair's, which was curled up into an angry little fist.

Weren't she and Marcus supposed to be in love? Why wasn't he undressing her in his elegant Edwardian bedroom? Why did he want to pal around with his nag of a cousin? Why wasn't he *at least* playing footsie with her beneath the table?

She squinted at Marcus, looking for a sign, some hint of his true feelings. A wide grin spread across his clean-shaven face and his green eyes sparkled with merriment. He seemed completely oblivious. Just having the time of his life in the warm summer sun. Blair sighed. Maybe she was being nasty and judgmental. She glanced at Camilla. Maybe she'd disappear soon, and she and Marcus could have sex beneath a hare-shaped conifer.

"The time of my life," Blair snapped.

"I daresay I'm *starved*," Lord Marcus exclaimed, rolling up the sleeves on his white linen button-down before taking a seat at the glass-topped table. He reached for a tiny silver platter that was laden with delicate cucumber sandwiches and popped a triangle in his mouth.

"You're always hungry when I'm around," Camilla giggled. She poked him in the belly and sipped her martini delicately.

"Remember that time I came to visit you at Yale and we went to that gorgeous little town in Vermont for a weekend ski?" Camilla turned to Blair. "We were on the slopes all day and all I wanted was a nice soak in the tub. When I got out, Marcus had ordered everything—*everything!*—off the room service menu so we could eat by the fire."

Blair was overcome with the urge to grab her mallet and smack Camilla over the head. She looked at Marcus, who was blushing. Maybe he and Camilla were the kind of cousins who liked to play doctor. Even after they were too old to play. Didn't Horseface realize *she* was Marcus's girlfriend?

"Oh, Cam, I'm sure Blair doesn't want to hear about our ski weekend." Marcus stood up, waving the empty sandwich plate at the butler.

Blair stood up, too. "Anyone up for another game, set— whatever it's fucking called? Maybe I can take a turn this time."

"Oh, I think I'm all worn out. I ought to have warned you," Marcus apologized. "Camilla is an absolute whiz at games."

Well, fine then. "Speaking of whiz," Blair muttered under her breath. "I need the loo." She'd picked up quite a few Britishisms in the last couple of days.

"Oh my." Camilla blushed. "There's that Yank wit."

And there's that Brit bitchiness.

"Just inside," Lord Marcus instructed. "Through the library and on your left."

"I'll find it," huffed Blair, stumbling a little as she started toward the house. The gin had gone straight to her head. "Don't get up."

She clopped along the flagstone path, smoothing the wrinkles in the white Thomas Pink shirtdress she'd changed into especially for their afternoon of lawn games. The house was surprisingly cluttered and smelled of rotting flowers. Of course the furniture was beautiful and the rugs especially so—apparently Lady Rhodes sent a buyer to Marrakech every other year to add to her collection. But a stained-glass window in the library made the house feel oddly churchlike, and Blair felt strange wandering around alone, knowing Lady Rhodes was upstairs somewhere nursing a hangover.

Alone in the powder room, she lit another Silk Cut, her new favorite English cigarette, and studied her reflection in the gilt-framed mirror as she exhaled. She narrowed her eyes and tucked in her chin, practicing the sexy look she'd fix on her boyfriend. One more drink and she'd suggest heading back to Claridge's for a late-afternoon romp. Lawn games were all well and good, but she was in the mood for some *real* exercise. She smoked the entire cigarette and pocketed a piece of the Beaton-Rhodes French-milled shell-shaped soap just because.

Old habits never die.

Outside, a new batch of martinis had been mixed, and Lord Marcus offered a fresh glass to Blair as she took her seat.

"She'll want an ashtray," Camilla quipped, nervously eyeing the inch of ash at the tip of Blair's cigarette.

"I'll use the lawn, thanks," Blair replied flatly, taking a swig from her paper-thin Riedel glass, spilling only a little on the table in the process.

"Darling, wait," Lord Marcus jovially reprimanded her. "We're having a toast. We were waiting for you."

"What's the occasion?" asked Blair, holding in a burp.

"While you were inside, Camilla gave me the most wonderful news."

She's going to Switzerland to get her enormous nose fixed? She's finally coming out of the closet as a big fat dyke? She's decided to become a nun?

"She's extending her stay. She'll be with us all summer long. Isn't that glorious?" Lord Marcus clinked his glass against hers.

Camilla took a dainty sip of her drink and put her hand protectively over Blair's.

"We'll be such good friends, we'll be almost like sisters," she promised, this time sounding more like the evil witchy stepmother who wants to eat Hansel and Gretel than one of the three little pigs.

Blair smiled tightly and drained her glass quickly before turning back to Camilla. "I always wanted an *older* sister."

Marcus wrapped his squash-toned arms around the two of them and squeezed them into a group hug. "I knew you two would get along."

He kissed them each on the cheek, and Blair closed her eyes, trying to pretend Camilla wasn't there.

Thank goodness she's always had a vivid imagination.

a star is born (sort of)

Serena's bright orange Hermès rubber flip-flops thwacked noisily against the black-and-white-checked marble floor of the Chelsea Hotel hallway as she made her way to room 609, where Ken Mogul was putting up her costar, Thaddeus Smith. The Chelsea was probably the most famous hotel in New York City. Home to iconic artists like Andy Warhol and rock stars like Janis Joplin, it had once suffered a terrible fire and all its famous residents had been forced out. Now it was mostly a tourist trap, but it still had a historic sixties allure, and its basement housed a dark, trendy bar, aptly named Serena.

Serena couldn't understand why Thaddeus got to stay in a hotel and she had to live in a shabby apartment with no A/C. She'd been sitting alone, too hot to move, since Jason left, when Ken had called and told her to come down for an impromptu rehearsal with Thad. Serena took a deep breath, fiddled nervously with the zippers on her gunmetal gray Balenciaga motorcycle bag, and knocked on the chipped door to room 609.

"Hi, you!" she squealed happily when Vanessa Abrams opened the door. It had only been a little over two weeks since graduation, but it felt like this was their twentieth reunion or something. Vanessa was wearing a black silk jersey wrap dress and the coolest silver flat sandals Serena had ever seen. "You look amazing!"

Vanessa opened her mouth to respond but was interrupted

by Ken. "Serena," he called slowly. He was perched on the windowsill inside the large main room of the hotel suite, smoking an unfiltered cigarette. "Welcome to our universe!"

"Nice to see you again." Serena giggled as she stepped through the door and crossed the room, which was flooded with light from Twenty-third Street. The walls were painted an astringent mint green that reminded her of the dorm bathrooms at Hanover Academy, the New Hampshire boarding school where she'd spent her junior year. There was an overstuffed brown couch with cracks and splits in the leather along the armrests, and dozens of little potted cactuses lined the windowsill. Serena could see an unmade king-size bed through the French doors.

"You can kind of picture all the people who've had sex here, can't you?" Vanessa whispered. Serena wrinkled her nose. Now she could.

"You know Vanessa, of course." Ken tossed his cigarette out of the open window behind him. "I've asked her to come aboard as our director of photography."

Not like she had any choice.

"Great, cool." Serena winked at Vanessa, who was now busying herself with some serious-looking equipment.

"And I'm Thaddeus," a sexy voice announced as the star strolled in from the adjacent bedroom.

Thaddeus Smith was taller than Serena had expected, and his thick dirty blond hair stood on end, giving him an extra inch or so. He was wearing an unremarkable outfit of dark jeans and a faded black Lacoste polo, collar standing up with a sort of dorky deliberateness. Serena had the impression that she already knew him, and in a way she did: she'd watched him romance a sweet-faced Southern starlet in the two romantic comedies they'd done together, she'd seen him flee a homicidal maniac (who turned out to be his long-lost twin brother, also played by him in a challenging dual role). She'd even seen him in a skintight white bodysuit, playing a mute otherworldly creature awakened by the sun's alignment with an ancient Mayan ruin. She'd heard that familiar baritone before, as he flirted and bantered on the talk shows, and of course she'd scoped out his signature abs in countless Les Best underwear advertisements. In person, he more than lived up to the hype: he was gorgeous, from the golden stubble on the sharp planes of his face to his tanned and perfect feet.

Thaddeus took Serena's hand in his and shook it firmly. "It's so great to meet you at last." His light blue eyes locked with her dark blue ones, or was she just imagining it?

"You too," she breathed.

"I'm glad we're all here, now," Ken began, lighting another cigarette. He hugged his knees to his chest, perching on the windowsill in his slippery-looking royal-blue bicycle shorts. "Scripts out. And Thaddeus, from now on she's Holly, not Serena."

Thaddeus plopped down on the cracked leather sofa, tossing the throw pillows carelessly onto the floor. "Have a seat, Holly."

Serena dug into her bag to retrieve her script, then sat on the couch, resisting the urge to immediately snuggle closer to her costar.

Because *that* just wouldn't be professional.

Ken closed his eyes and breathed in deeply, his nostrils flaring. He spread his fingers out in front of him like insect feelers, hopped off the windowsill, and staggered toward the center of the room. His eyes popped open when he bumped into the chipped wooden coffee table and a mountain of script rewrites slid to the floor. Then he leapt onto the table and crouched on its edge, leaning in very close to the twosome. "We're going to start with the big climax. This is the emotional heart of the movie and I want to nail this before we get to any of the other stuff. Everything builds to this moment."

Ken was crouched so close Serena could smell his dank-cigarette breath. She held up her script as a barrier and started to page through it. She'd assumed they'd read from the beginning. She knew her lines in the first few scenes but was a little shaky on the second half of the movie.

"So we'll read through once and then let's get up, get moving, find our space in the room, and get this going, okay? Vanessa's going to roll, just to shoot some test footage so you guys can study up on it later. Sound good?" Ken asked, still crouching like a gargoyle on the coffee table.

"Let's go," nodded Thaddeus, tossing his script aside.

"Almost ready," interjected Vanessa, who was linking her handheld camera to one of the director's laptops.

"And Holly?" asked Ken, resting his chin on his hand while his finger appeared to be up his nose.

"Ready when you are," Serena muttered. Shit, shit! She didn't know a single line. She took a deep breath.

"Darling. You're always rescuing me. How can I ever repay you?" she began, waving her right hand slowly, deliberately. It felt like a sexy mannerism. A little flair.

"You don't have to repay me," replied Thaddeus as Jeremy Stone, in his famously sexy baritone. They were standing by the window, and he leaned in close, the afternoon sun hitting his rugged profile as he took Serena by the wrist. "It's me who should repay you. I owe you everything, Holly. You showed me how to be . . ." He paused intently. "You showed me how to be me."

Maybe it was because he was a talented actor, or maybe it was because he was just gorgeous, but somehow he made the dorky dialogue sound almost normal. He was standing so close to Serena she could smell mint on his breath. Was he really just perfect?

Yup.

"I . . . I . . . " Serena faltered. "I just don't know what to say."

Across the room, behind the camera, Vanessa cleared her throat.

"Don't say anything," Thaddeus-as-Jeremy cooed. "Just stand still and let me look at you."

Serena didn't move. She couldn't help but believe everything Thaddeus was saying.

"I'm going to stop you here," announced Ken Mogul. "Holly, babes, remember: you're *not* Serena. You're Holly."

"Okay," Serena whispered. She didn't feel like Holly Golightly. She felt like herself and like the perfect guy was right in front of her. She'd spent her whole life not acting fake around guys: it was kind of hard to *act* around one, especially one so . . . cute.

"And quit with that hand stuff," Ken whined, sounding like a big baby. "Looks like you're swatting away mosquitoes."

"Sorry." Through the open window Serena could hear the sound of traffic whizzing by. She kind of wished she were out there instead, window shopping on Mercer Street in Soho with Thaddeus or maybe letting him feed her sushi on the roof of Sushi Samba, just a few blocks downtown. Thaddeus leaned out of the large window and inhaled deeply. Was he reading her mind?

"Just listen to Thad," Ken continued with his finger still up his nose. "He's not Thad, anymore—is he? No, he's Jeremy. You hear that—his shyness? His nervousness? He's terrified of you, you see. Terrified and enchanted. Make us all feel that, okay? Make us all fall in love with you."

Like that was ever difficult before.

"Let's go again." Ken clapped his hands while simultaneously lighting another cigarette, even though his last one had burned to ash without his even touching it.

Thaddeus snapped back to attention, leaning in close to Serena again.

"Darling. You're always rescuing me. How can I ever repay you?" she asked, more assuredly this time.

"You don't have to repay me."

"You must come to my . . ." She couldn't remember the rest of the line. She *had* to glance at her script.

"Party!" cried Ken. "*Party!* Haven't you read the script, Holly?"

"Yeah," muttered Serena defensively, resisting the urge to kick the pile of script rewrites on the floor up and out the large, bright window.

"Okay, let's skip ahead a little bit." Ken rubbed his weirdly red forehead. "Let's do the big morning scene. There's just a little dialogue there, so you should be able to manage that, right, Holly?"

"Sure." She felt like she was doing everything wrong, even though she'd only said a few words. Wasn't there any time to get warmed up?

"Okay, Thaddeus, you begin," Ken directed, with his new cigarette torched in hand.

"Holly," Thaddeus recited, from memory—his script was still lying on the couch. "I knew I'd find you here."

"Will you always know where to find me?" Serena could see Ken shaking his head out of the corner of her eye, so she dropped her script onto the floor. She could do this. She stood on tiptoe and leaned into Thaddeus's broad chest.

"I will if you stand still," he pronounced softly. "Never run away again."

"I promise," Serena whispered. It was her last line in the film. She craned her neck, lifting her face to her costar's, offering herself up to him. She could smell toothpaste and nicotine on Thaddeus's warm breath, Kiehl's oatmeal lotion on his hands, and Tide on his clothes. She was barely touching him, just resting her hands against his firm chest, but she could feel his body against hers, from his strong, broad back to his perfect abs, from his lean and muscled forearms to his flip-flopped feet. And she could feel something else: a flicker of electricity in the air, in the tiny pocket of space between their two bodies. Was this acting or was it real?

"Okay," Thaddeus stammered. He took a step back and Serena, who had been leaning all of her weight on him, stumbled a bit.

He laughed nervously. "Ken, a smoke?"

Ken held out a pack of Marlboro Reds and Thaddeus selected one and coolly lit it.

"What'd you think, Ken?" he asked, looping his thumb in his waistband.

"Good. Better. I felt more spark that last time. But Holly needs to pick up the slack. Holly, we can do some rewrites if you're having trouble with your lines."

"What do you mean?" Serena sank into the worn couch. She hadn't made *too* many mistakes, had she?

"If there are too many words, you know," he explained, pronouncing the words loudly and slowly, like he was speaking to someone whose English wasn't so good. "If you're having trouble remembering all of them."

Was he calling her *stupid?*

"No, it's fine," she sighed wearily.

"She'll get the hang of it." Thaddeus sat down beside her. He rested his soft hand on her bare knee, giving her leg a supportive squeeze.

You know I will, Serena agreed silently. God, was she already in love? Sometimes she was almost too easy.

No comment.

"Of course, of course," agreed Ken. "We just need some more rehearsal time, I think. What do you think, Vanessa?"

Vanessa hadn't even caught everything on camera because they hadn't given her enough time to set up her equipment. "It rocked," she lied enthusiastically. After all, it was only rehearsal.

And by the looks of things, they were going to need *lots* more of them.

you think you know someone

"Honey, I'm hoooome!" Dan stuck his head into the doorway of his little sister Jenny's bedroom. "Vanessa?"

"Hey." Vanessa stood up from behind Jenny's painting easel. The cozy room was still lined with Jenny's canvases—washed-out landscapes, architectural drawings of famous New York buildings like the Dakota on Seventy-second Street, some nude portraits Vanessa saw Dan avert his eyes from just in case they were his sister's *self*-portraits. She wrapped her arms around Dan's skinny frame and squeezed. "Thank you so much for letting me stay here."

"It'll be great," he assured her, plopping down on the blue-flannel-duvet-covered bed. "We'll make it our Big New York Summer. I've been thinking all about it. All the things we'll do together—pedaling those stupid boats in Central Park, bagels from H&H Bagels on our days off—"

"Um, that sounds great, but I'm going to be really busy with work, you know? It's going to take a lot of work to get this movie right." She nodded toward the computer screen where Serena van der Woodsen's ethereal face was paused, her eyes half closed. She was reviewing the rehearsal footage from this afternoon, and if it was any indication of what the finished film would look like—well, it wasn't pretty.

"Right." Dan pouted a little. "Of course."

On the up side, the longer Serena fumbled through her

rehearsals, the more time Vanessa had to experiment with her camera work. She was going to give him something better. She was determined to do something truly avant-garde and unusual, something that would really wow Ken Mogul and his producers. He'd mentioned Godard. But she was the master of mixing humor with tragedy. She would show the used condom stuck to Holly's shoe, the tarnished side of the party princess!

"Where's your dad?" she asked, changing the subject. It was only a matter of time before she ran into Dan's Beat poet dad, Rufus, wearing his usual stained Mets T-shirt and too-snug tan cargo shorts. She was hoping to see him before they had a middle-of-the-night run-in. Who knew what he'd be wearing then?

He shrugged. "You talk to Ruby?" He dug into his pockets and retrieved a battered old pack of Camels, lit one, and then lay back on Jenny's lumpy, narrow bed. "I hope you guys made up. Life's too short, you know?"

"Huh?" Vanessa asked lazily, lying down next to him. Ruby had sent a couple of apologetic text messages, but Vanessa was too mad to bother reading them all the way through. She could imagine Ruby squeezing Piotr's back zits while they did it in his paint-splattered studio—aka her old room. She snuggled her almost-bald head into Dan's ropy neck and whispered, "I can't really deal with it now, you know?"

"That's too bad," he observed solemnly. "I always admired your relationship."

"Sure." She couldn't resist giggling a little. "Are you feeling okay?"

Dan turned toward her so their noses were almost touching. Vanessa kissed his smoky-tasting lips. He touched her face. "You know, I never realized it before, but happiness is, like, right there in front of you, you know what I mean? It's like us—like you're all I need to be happy, and you're right here, in my house. I mean, I know you'll have to work a lot and everything, but it's so great. It's actually so much easier to achieve happiness than it is to embrace ugliness."

Vanessa bit her lip. She loved Dan, but she really hoped he wasn't about to pull another embarrassing proclamation of undying devotion like he had at his own graduation. Some things were better left unsaid.

You can say that again.

"Did you learn that on the job?" she teased. "I didn't know they offered free New Age self-help lectures at the Strand."

"I'm not talking about work." He sucked on his Camel hard and defensively. "I read *Siddhartha* during my break this afternoon. Life's just so short. . . . I mean, we can only hope to find some meaning in this life, you know?"

The only book Vanessa knew him to have spoken as passionately about was *The Sorrows of Young Werther*, a creepy book about a moody, depressive guy who kills himself in the end because his girlfriend marries someone else.

"All right, I'm officially confused. What the hell are you talking about?" she asked. Her eyebrows furrowed as she looked into his light brown eyes.

"I'm talking about the meaning of life," he replied simply.

Or was he talking about a certain perfectly perky round-butted blonde?

hey people!

I've discovered something very important about myself: I'm totally bi. It's not what you're thinking—I'm just torn between where I want to spend my summer and I've decided I really want to have it both ways. Thank God for Teterboro Airport. A quick drive to the runway and I'm on the island in less than an hour. That gives me a chance to ogle the surfer boys and say yes to every party I'm invited to here at home.

There's something so exclusive about parties in the city during the summer. So intimate, with no unwanted guests. Well, almost. Not that we don't like to have our picture taken; we'd just like to make sure our beach hair doesn't have any actual sand in it before the flash goes off. Yes, I'm talking about the paparazzi. Obviously they have to work all summer, and obviously they're bored because they've been hounding the few celebs in town—me included—like every night was an MTV Music Awards after-party at Lindsay's loft.

But summer and the beach go hand in hand, and I could never completely forsake the shore, but that heartthrob actor T has done just that, abandoning his lavish spread on the North Shore (yes, the one you saw on that episode of *Cribs*) to spend a steaming-hot summer in sticky New York City. Now that's dedication.

across the pond

I know we started out as an English colony, but we won the war (no hard feelings!) and therefore we do things a bit differently

on this side of the pond. I like the whole royalty thing—
especially a certain heir to the throne and his party-monster
redheaded younger brother—but there's a lot about the English
that I just don't understand. For example, I hear that a certain
young, foxy, blue-eyed American girl we all know and love has
gotten herself mixed up with a titled gentleman who seems to
have eyes for his, um, cousin? Apparently, in some grand old
English families it's perfectly acceptable to ask your cousin
to move in for the summer, to hold her hand during intimate
dinners at London's finest restaurants, to slip away together to
the thatch-roofed country house for a weekend foxhunt. How's
that for culture shock?

your e-mail

Q: Dear GG,
My mom insisted that I take an internship at a glossy
magazine this summer. She says it'll help prepare me
for the real world, but I feel like I'm the only one spending
my summer cooped up inside the fashion closet, packing
next season's Marc Jacobs shoes into boxes and keeping
track of the Me&Ro jewelry. It's like working in retail,
and besides, I have the rest of my life to work, don't I?
Shouldn't I be chilling at the beach with my babelicious
boyfriend or something?
—In the Closet

A: Dear In the Closet,
How do you think I feel? I'm still here, albeit with the A/C
cranked and a chilled bottle of Dom next to the computer,
hard at work, serving all your gossip needs. But seriously:
help yourself to something Guccilicious from the sunglass
drawer. You deserve it! (And no one will notice if you throw
something in for your boyfriend, too.)
—GG

Q: Dear GG,
Does that guy **N** have a long-lost brother? I think I saw him at the Oyster Shack on the Island, but it couldn't have been the same guy; this guy was dressed like a construction worker and hanging out with some skanky-looking but undeniably hot townie chick. Any idea what's going on?
—Double Take

A: Dear Double Take,
There's definitely only one **N**. If he's in the construction game now, I suggest you hire him to come over and build you a deck. Maybe he'll work up a sweat and then you can invite him to go skinny-dipping!
—GG

sightings

B getting into a tiff with the mousy-looking handbag clerk at Harvey Nichols. They've got waiting lists in London, too, but some girls have never learned that patience is a virtue. **S** wandering around an unfamiliar part of the Upper East Side—really far from the park —looking forlorn and buying Purina cat chow at the deli. Maybe she's trying some crazy new diet? **N** strolling along Catachungo Road in Hampton Bays, wearing a Yale baseball cap and standing quite close to a mystery girl wearing a pink tube top embellished with Old Navy logos. I must have missed their Hamptons store opening. **V** settling into a maroon leather barber chair at an old-school barbershop on the Upper West Side, ignoring the men-only rule. Maybe someone should tell her that she's definitely not in Brooklyn anymore. **D** curled up on a bench in Union Square, reading a thick paperback book on kundalini yoga while smoking a cigarette. Is he planning to write an epic poem about yoga positions for lung cancer patients? Who wants to know? I know I do.

And you know you love me.

gossip girl

townies are people too

Nate guided his trusty Schwinn off the gravelly road and onto the dirt shoulder in front of the Oyster Shack, managing to avoid a replay of his humiliating wipeout yesterday. After their ice cream, Tawny had taken him to get his tire fixed at Bob's Gas 'n' Dogs and it was as good as new. He breathed in the fresh air appreciatively. He'd only smoked a third of a joint that morning, so his head was clear.

That's a first.

Even though it was only six o'clock, the Oyster Shack was crowded with kids in shorts and halter tops eating fries and drinking canned Bud. Leaning the bike on the kickstand, Nate ambled over to the barn-red picnic bench where Tawny sat smoking a Virginia Slim, a devilish little smile on her full, opalescent peach–glossed lips.

Normally Nate would have felt kind of stupid meeting a girl on a bike, but he kind of enjoyed the workout, the breeze in his face and the wind in his hair. Of course, he could enjoy the wind in his hair behind the wheel of his dad's powder blue 1978 vintage Aston Martin convertible parked in his garage only twenty minutes away, but the car was the Captain's pride and joy, and Nate wasn't allowed to drive it alone, much less into one of the Hamptons' less desirable neighborhoods, like Hampton Bays.

After they'd shared an innocent ice cream cone and gotten

Nate's bike fixed yesterday, Tawny had suggested they meet up for dinner today. Nate hardly needed convincing; like a good ex-girlfriend, Fate always pulled through for him, right when he needed her. Just when his loneliness had started to get him down, he'd happened to meet confident, sexy Tawny.

"You made it," she chirped, stubbing her cigarette out on the table and tossing the butt in the grass behind her. She was wearing a peach-colored bikini top and a black jersey wrap-around skirt that showed off her tanned, round, but firm thighs. Her hair was down, grazing her freckled shoulders, and her peachy lips matched the bikini straps that were falling off her shoulders. "Without falling."

"Yeah, no accidents this time." Nate laughed, shaking his head. He flipped down the collar of the clean but faded light blue Brooks Brothers shirt he'd changed into after work and slipped onto the bench across from her. "So I'd say the day is going pretty well."

"How was work?" Tawny asked as she smeared some goopy vanilla-scented stuff on her lips. Nate could smell it from where he sat.

"Just the usual: backbreaking manual labor." He'd spent all of yesterday and today nailing new shingles onto Coach Michaels's roof. His hands were riddled with calluses and his arms ached. "I'm working for my coach, so it's not like I can slack off. He's kind of an asshole. I guess it's just like practice."

Only without the stick. And the ball. And the rest of the team.

"You must really like him, though, to want to work for him all summer," Tawny countered.

Nate shrugged, rubbing his hand over his stiff neck. "I guess." No need to tell her about the stolen Viagra and the withheld diploma, right?

Best not.

"Poor boy," she cooed. "Maybe you need a massage. I can practice on you. I'm totally going to be an LMT after I graduate."

"A what?" He had no idea what she was talking about. LMT? Low-class mega-slut townie?

"A *licensed massage therapist,* silly! I can't believe you didn't know that. Anyway, I talked to these people at this spa in Sag Harbor and they might let me do an actual internship. You know, practicing on real people? I'm so psyched." She leaned in across the table and began massaging Nate's forearm, using both of her hands and applying a surprising amount of pressure, her long manicured fingertips scraping his skin like ice scrapers on a car windshield. "See?" she asked. "Doesn't that feel good?"

It did feel good, sort of, but Nate was much more interested in the view: Tawny was leaning so far forward that her impressive pear-shaped boobs were totally visible.

"So, um, you're still in high school, then?" Nate mumbled, remembering that it was his turn to say something. "I just graduated." Saying that felt good. It made him feel manly.

Oh boy.

"I'm graduating next year," she explained, moving her hands from his forearm to his chest, which was tight from hammering. "I can't wait. I'm so sick of high school. I figure I'll get my certification, you know, get a house in the Bays. If you're good, you can make such awesome cash from the summer crowd you don't have to work the rest of the year. That's totally my plan: make a good living mooching off summer people." She laughed.

"Cool." Nate was having trouble concentrating on what Tawny was saying because her boobs were practically in his lap. He'd tuned her out so completely she sounded kind of like the parents in a Peanuts cartoon. *Wah-wah-wah-wah-wah.* Her lips looked so full and peach-colored and shiny, and she smelled like vanilla.

He pitched his head forward and lightly kissed her, touching her cheeks gently. Her mouth tasted like Diet Coke and some sort of artificial but totally delicious fruit.

After a few moments she giggled and pulled away. "We can do that all night, but I want to know about your plans too," she went on, sitting back down and taking his hand. "You can tell me all about it over dinner."

"Sure, yeah." Nate stood and patted his pocket to make sure he'd remembered to bring his wallet. He wondered if the Oyster Shack accepted platinum American Express. He licked his lips, which tasted sort of slick and fruity now themselves and would probably make his beer taste like piña colada. "Let's get something to eat and I'll tell you my whole master plan."

Nate Archibald has a master plan?

"Sounds impressive." Tawny giggled again as she stood and gathered up her cigarettes, her lighter, and her gold pleather XOXO clutch with buckles all over it.

"Well, I'm starting Yale in a couple of months—"

"*Yale?* Really? Damn, that's a good school." She linked her arm with Nate's. "And expensive."

Then again, education is like a Birkin bag—how can you put a price on such things?

b is for betrothed

Blair Waldorf crossed her legs and leaned back in the deep-brown high-backed leather chair. Lifting the white Spode porcelain teacup to her lips, she took a dainty sip of lukewarm Earl Grey tea and smiled at Jemima, the salesgirl who was hovering over her. "Miss Waldorf," Jemima tittered, handing Blair a small navy blue leather portfolio. "Whenever you're ready."

Blair opened the book; inside were her black American Express card, a receipt, and a pen, which she grabbed, signing the dotted line without glancing at it.

"Lovely. Now, I've had your parcels packed up and they'll be off to Claridge's shortly. Can I do anything else for you? Fetch a taxi, perhaps?"

"No, thank you." She smiled gracefully. "I think I'll walk."

She had been sitting comfortably in a private back room in a new boutique called Kid in West London for an hour, keeping Jemima, a pretty brunette with terrible teeth, busy fetching every style of boot they stocked. As she tried on the twenty-plus pairs of boots, she'd had two cups of tea, glanced at the new issue of French *Vogue*, and made a telephone call to Lord Marcus. Voicemail. She wondered if he was working, or if he was off with Camilla somewhere, buying new croquet mallets, or . . .

Or *what?*

Blair didn't give up easily and she was determined not to let yesterday get her down. Maybe Marcus and Camilla needed to get their cousinly bonding thing out of the way. They'd undoubtedly soon tire of each other's company. Besides, Marcus was likely to forget Camilla's *name* when he caught a glimpse of Blair in her new knee-high black python-skin boots and her new black lace Gossard corset and matching boy shorts, which she planned on modeling for him that very night in between courses during the champagne-and-chocolate room service dinner she'd planned.

Tucking the still-warm credit card back into her new Smythson billfold, Blair dropped her wallet inside the limited-edition hand-painted Goyard bag she'd picked up the day before and walked out of the store and onto the quiet stretch of Press Street. She'd been to London only once with her family, when she was twelve. They'd stayed at the Langham Hotel just off Regent Street, visited Old Ben and Buckingham Palace, seen the crown jewels, watched the changing of the guard, drunk tea, and eaten scones. As far as she could remember, she'd spent most of the trip listening to Madonna on her iPod. But that was London as a *tourist*. Now that she *lived* here, things were totally different.

Everyone said London was gray, overcast, foggy, and depressing, but it had been clear and sunny all week. The trees were in full bloom, there were lush gardens on every block, and every building was ornate and beautiful. Everyone also said that the English were standoffish, with bad teeth and thick accents, and although their teeth and accents *were* distractions, so far every person Blair had spoken to had been unfailingly polite.

Of course they had been—she'd only talked to salespeople who worked on commission.

Blair checked her cell again: no messages. She tossed the phone back into her bag. She understood that a gentleman had to pay extra attention to his guest—family was very important to the English upper class—and Camilla was lovely, really. She really was. Even if she did look like a blond cartoon freakworm. And Blair understood, really she did. But she was ready to spice things up a little, and the more Lord Marcus made her wait, the more fidgety and eager she got. Maybe the whole thing was just a ploy to turn her on as much as possible?

Um, maybe.

Strolling down the street in the general direction of her hotel, Blair felt like a cross between Julia Roberts in *Pretty Woman*—the scene where she goes shopping in a giant black wide-brimmed hat and has all the Rodeo Drive salespeople waiting on her hand and foot—and Audrey Hepburn in *My Fair Lady*, the beautiful Cockney waif who rises from obscurity on the streets of London to become the toast of the town. Except Blair was neither a prostitute nor a waif from the gutter.

Details, details.

She glanced up and down the street, but every store window, every awning, looked familiar. Had she really made it to *all* the stores in the neighborhood? Finding great clothes in London was easy, and the exchange rate made it even better. Blair noticed it the minute she arrived; she had to get cash for a taxi and was surprised at how many bright, pretty pastel-colored bills she got in exchange for her boring old U.S. dollars. The teller at the bank even gave her a handful of change—including an oversize penny that was worth two cents, not just one, a funny hexagon-shaped coin, and a bunch of thick, heavy coins that were worth a whole pound each. If the English used coins for the same thing Americans used bills for, clearly this was a place to find great bargains. Not that she *needed* to find bargains.

Blair was standing outside of what at first looked like just another West London brick mansion: a tall, well-lit town house with big, clean windows and blooming flower boxes underneath them. A lifetime of shopping had given Blair a sixth sense; she just *knew* when something good was lurking nearby. Through the street-level windows she could see an ornate Chinese vase stuffed full of white camellias on a pretty gilded table. Blair couldn't see any clothes but she was absolutely convinced something incredible was inside.

After all, everyone has a special talent.

She rang the doorbell and the door buzzed back, so she pushed it open and stepped into the marble foyer of the elegant house. The open, airy parlor floor was filled with simple displays: an incredible Kelly green crocodile bowling bag perched on top of a broken Corinthian column bathed in the soft glow of a spotlight, a show-stopping pair of red velvet ballerina flats atop a satin pillow. They were so plush Blair couldn't resist stroking them. A tall Indian girl with long, thick hair smiled at her from behind the antique art nouveau desk. Blair felt a little self-conscious in her Rock & Republic jeans, her gold silk Eberjey camisole and her skimpy sandals, but she wasn't about to walk out.

"I'm Lyla," the salesgirl chirped in a clipped English accent. "Do let me know if I can help you find anything."

Blair walked to the foot of the gracefully curving staircase. Sensing something in the distance, she ascended the marble steps grandly. The steps were *exactly* like the ones Eliza descends in *My Fair Lady*, in the scene where she has her society debut.

See, life really does imitate art.

The second floor was nearly empty, except for a floor-to-ceiling three-way mirror against the far wall. Sun flooded in and Blair paused, pretending it was her own private dressing room. In the middle of the space, suspended from a glass hanger, hung a long white dress. It was made of silk, cut along the bias, and seemed to breathe as if it had a life of its own. It was . . . *beautiful*. Whoever wore that dress would be the star of a never-ending love story with herself. Blair reached out to touch the dress, transfixed. Could it be? It was.

It was a wedding dress.

It was *her* wedding dress.

"Would you like to try it on?"

Blair whirled around to see Lyla from downstairs. She hadn't heard her coming.

"Yes, definitely," Blair half whispered. "I think I'm going to need it."

For what, exactly?

The shop only accommodated one customer at a time, so there was no need for dressing rooms. Lyla explained this, reaching up to remove the glass hanger from its tack on the wall, while Blair all but leapt out of her clothes. She grabbed the gown and slid into it headfirst. The chiffon was as soft and light as fresh whipped cream, and she shivered as it fell down the length of her body.

Avoiding the mirror until everything was perfect, Blair stood by the windows, looking down onto the lush private garden behind the store.

"Here, let's put this on as well." Lyla held up a delicate gold lariat necklace and slipped it around Blair's neck. "I think you're ready to have a look now," she murmured, turning Blair so that she faced the mirror.

Blair crossed the room carefully, holding the dress up so she didn't trip on the delicate hem. There was a small platform in front of the mirror and she stepped up onto it, avoiding her reflection until she was perfectly situated. She let go of the dress, shook her hair back from her face, and then gazed at her reflection.

"Oooh!" she gasped.

There it was: the future. Blair had never seen a more perfect dress in her life. It was so amazing, its beauty rubbed off on her. She wasn't even wearing proper makeup, but her face had never looked more flawless. She was wearing the wrong bra but her breasts had never looked so full. She felt like she'd stepped off the cover of *Town & Country*'s summer wedding issue. That old theory—that you just *know*, somehow, when you've found the right wedding dress—seemed to be true.

They'd be married in St. Patrick's on Fifth Avenue and they'd rent all the rooms in the St. Clair for the guests to stay in and for the reception. Her father would give her away with tears in his blue eyes, whispering, "I love you, Bear," as he handed her off to Marcus. Marcus would hold her hand throughout the ceremony in that intimate way of his, reminding her that they weren't just passionately in love, they were best friends.

"It's really quite something, isn't it?" Lyla crossed her arms in front of her. She was standing behind Blair, smiling approvingly. Blair met her gaze in the mirror.

"It's just perfect," she breathed, her eyes transfixed on the endless train of pure white silk.

"Have you set a date?"

Um, how about a proposal first? And what about, you know, college?

"I'll take it," Blair declared.

"Of course," Lyla agreed. "You won't be sorry. He's going to love it."

Blair nodded back hypnotically, still staring at her own reflection.

"And what about the necklace?" Lyla queried.

Why not? Blair thought.

Oh, yes, why not?

there's something about danny

The single complaint Dan had about his job at the Strand was that the bookstore lacked one essential, modern amenity: air-conditioning. This morning he was stationed in the completely airless basement, manning the information desk and keeping an eye on special orders, like the request for a skin diseases photo calendar. After a couple of torturous hours, he was definitely ready for some fresh air.

If that's what you call a smoke.

As soon as his replacement—a scowling, silent guy named Brent who'd worked at the store for about twenty years—arrived to take his place, Dan jogged up the narrow staircase and outside. A concrete ledge ran alongside the square beige building and he perched on it, enjoying the shade as he lit up.

The sidewalk was crowded with passersby browsing the Strand's large outdoor carts, which were full of super-discounted books no one wanted, like *Collectible Coins from Contemporary Canada* and *Tiger: The True Story of the Dog Who Loved a Cat*. Dan closed his eyes and tuned out the chatter of the bargain hunters. He took a deep drag on his cigarette and thought about Herman Hesse's *Siddhartha*. *"Love stirred in the hearts of the young daughters of the Brahmins when Siddhartha passed through the city streets, with his radiant brow, with his imperial glance, with his slender hips."* Dan couldn't help wanting to be Siddhartha, or at least be more *like* him.

He wished he had someone he could discuss it with, especially since his attempt to chat about it with Vanessa had ended so badly.

A tap on his shoulder interrupted his reverie. He opened his eyes.

"Dan?" Bree stood before him like a fit, blond daughter of a Brahmin, admiring him in all his Siddharthaness.

Who says wishes don't come true?

"Hi." He stood quickly. Bree was wearing a form-fitting green tank top and white spandex shorts. Her blond hair was in two tidy pigtails and her skin had a bold, healthy glow.

"Are you smoking?" she demanded, aghast.

"Uh, no." Dan dropped the lit cigarette to the ground and stubbed it out quickly. "I was holding it for this guy Steve. He had to run back inside."

Nice play, Shakespeare.

"Whew," she exhaled, fanning the air with her hands. "Smoking is just terrible for you."

"Oh, I know," Dan agreed earnestly, wiping his hands on his faded green cords. "It's really bad."

"I'm so glad I ran into you!" Bree hopped up onto the ledge and started swinging her legs like a kid who has to pee but doesn't want to get off the swing. "I wanted to tell you how much I liked *Siddhartha*."

"Yeah? That's great. I was actually just rereading it myself."

"Really? What a funny coincidence!"

Right. Coincidence.

"So you thought the book was interesting?" Dan asked, crossing his legs in a way he hoped looked quasi-intellectual and quasi-athletic. "What are you thinking of reading next?"

"Well, I'm going to read a book my yogi has been working on. It's about improving the way the brain communicates with the other organs in the body by meditating and doing yoga and chanting. There are, like, fifty chapters and most of them are a hundred pages long. He's been writing it for, like, eleven years, and he's going to try and have it published this year and he asked me to look at it for him. Me! Imagine! It's such an honor."

An honor? Sounds more like a pain in her well-yogacized ass.

"Anyway, I have to confess," she went on, looking Dan right in the eye. "I didn't just come by to talk books."

"You didn't?"

She didn't?

Dan blushed and looked down at the ground, kicking idly at the cigarette butt he'd claimed wasn't his. He wished he had it back.

"No, I wanted to see if you'd be interested in getting together sometime. I know that might sound kind of forward, but you know, I'm a person who believes in taking chances. I believe that the universe rewards bold actions, don't you?"

Dan nodded eagerly.

"Anyway, I'm kind of lonely this summer. I grew up here in Greenwich Village but I was in boarding school out west, so I don't really know anyone in the city anymore. I'm going to UC Santa Cruz in the fall, but I don't want to spend my last summer in the city all by myself."

"No, definitely not," Dan agreed. "I'd love to hang out."

"Awesome!" Bree cried, hopping down from the ledge. "What's your schedule like?"

"Well, I work days. So anytime after six."

"Cool. Do you think you'd be up for Bikram?"

"Sure," Dan nodded, even though he'd never heard of it. He didn't go out to clubs very often.

"Awesome!" she squealed again. "Give me your number and I'll call and confirm, but let's say Saturday?"

Dan recited his number and she typed it into her hot pink Razr. He had officially taken a much longer break than he was entitled to, but after Bree strolled away he had to light another Camel to calm his nerves. He wasn't quite sure what Bikram was—a trendy new nightclub? Some new Indian restaurant? Maybe it was a new underground independent film? But it didn't matter. Vanessa was busy filming, and he'd scored a hot date with a sweet, gorgeous girl who loved to read.

Oh, it's sure to be a hot date indeed.

lights, camera, but no action

"Cut!" barked Ken Mogul. "Fuck!" He threw his fluorescent green clipboard onto the floor and leapt out of the metal swivel chair he'd been slumped in. "Let's take ten, please. I need a fucking smoke."

Serena's hands trembled as she held the tip of her Gauloise cigarette to the flame from Thaddeus's silver Zippo. She inhaled deeply but the nicotine did little to calm her nerves. Memorizing her lines and reciting them properly had turned out to be harder than she thought. On top of everything, it was majorly scary to have Ken, freak show director extraordinaire, yelling at her every five seconds.

"Don't worry about him," Thaddeus assured her, running his hands through his dark blond curls and smiling at her with his adorable light blue eyes. He put his arm around Serena's shoulders and squeezed. "I know it's rough, and personally, I think you've done great for your first film. We're just on a tight schedule, you know, and he's nervous about pleasing the producers. Believe me, it has nothing to do with you."

It doesn't?

"Do you really think so?" Serena wondered, burrowing into Thaddeus's protective embrace. Normally she wouldn't have been quite so touchy-feely with a guy she'd only known for a couple of days, but Thaddeus wasn't your average guy. It was more than the simple fact that he was a movie star: they were pretending to be in love. They'd already kissed eight times for the stupid climax scene. Cuddling on the couch like old friends seemed natural.

"Listen up!" boomed the director, striding back into the room, tucking his pack of Marlboros into the chest pocket of his rumpled denim shirt, which, oddly enough, had the sleeves cut out, so it was really more of a vest than a shirt.

Serena shivered at the sound of his voice and Thaddeus put his hand protectively over hers.

"I lost it back there," Ken apologized. "Let's call it a day, shall we? Vanessa and I have to go over our shot list anyway, but I want you two to keep working. Go to dinner—it's on me."

"Thanks, Ken." Thaddeus stood and stretched, yawning noisily and giving off the heavenly odors of sweat and Carolina Herrera for Men cologne. "It really has been a long day. I could definitely use a drink."

"And this will give you a chance to work on your chemistry, right, Holly? Get to know your leading man. Talk to him, listen to him, learn from him. I really want to see you *meld*, okay?"

Serena nodded and stubbed her cigarette out in the mother-of-pearl ashtray perched precariously on the arm of the brown leather couch. She could meld, especially with Thaddeus, but maybe not while Ken was watching.

"Good," grunted the disgruntled director. "So go, have a bite. That's your homework."

Dinner with a major Hollywood hottie? Is there extra credit?

After gorging themselves on the city's best steak tartare— mixed with two delicate quail eggs and served with a healthy portion of sea-salt-encrusted French fries—Serena and Thaddeus emerged from As Such on Clinton Street, currently *the* coolest, most crowded spot for the summer. They'd shared a bottle of Veuve Clicquot and a molten chocolate cake with fresh huckleberries for dessert, and Serena had tipsily blurted out the story of how she'd wound up not getting asked back to Hanover Academy last fall.

She'd spent the summer in Europe, partying with her older brother, Erik, and flirting with Frenchmen. Erik had left for Brown in August, but Serena had stayed and stayed. School just seemed so boring and unnecessary when the beaches in Saint-Tropez were so inviting, even in September. Thankfully Constance Billard, the New York City all-girls private school she'd attended since kindergarten, had been kind enough to take her back.

"I'd sort of thought I was bound for community college and living with my parents for the rest of my life," she admitted. "Now here I am acting in this movie, living on my own, and going to Yale in the fall." She grinned drunkenly and a little seductively at Thaddeus. "I guess you just never know *what's* going to happen." Secretly, it was an invitation to kiss her. But they were in a crowded restaurant full of starers and gossips—it was probably best that he didn't.

"Should we go?" Thaddeus asked, as if he couldn't wait to take her somewhere more private.

As the pair stepped outside onto the crowded, steaming street corner, they were startled by a sudden, insistent cry.

"Thad! Thad!" A bulky, bearded figure emerged from the shadows wielding a camera. He snapped pictures as he hurried toward them, the bright flash illuminating the otherwise dark stretch of street.

Thaddeus put his arm protectively around Serena's waist, a phony but still charming smile plastered to his handsome face.

Serena smiled, too. She was used to having her photo taken for newspaper society columns. She'd even modeled a few times, but it felt a little scary to be hounded like this.

"Let's go," sighed Thaddeus. He waved at the photographer. "Okay, man, that's cool, that's enough. We're going."

But the guy trailed them, weaving and bobbing like a boxer, snapping and clicking the camera's shutter so quickly it sounded like machine gun fire. He finished a roll, deftly reloaded the camera in a matter of seconds, and kept shooting.

"That's enough," Thaddeus ordered, more firmly this time. He tugged on Serena's arm, pulling her across the street, "Come on. Let's go."

Serena continued to smile but her huge blue eyes darted around, searching for a cab.

"Who is she, Thad?" the photographer demanded from behind them. "What are you wearing tonight, Thad?" he continued in an almost mocking tone. "You're gorgeous, sweetheart. What about you? What are you wearing?"

Actually, she was wearing her favorite black Les Best pique cotton sundress and black Capezio ballet slippers, but she was too freaked out to open her mouth.

"That's enough, man!" Thaddeus yelled angrily.

Was he going to pull a Cameron Diaz?

Thaddeus stepped into the oncoming traffic on Clinton Street, waving his arms frantically like a survivor marooned on a desert island flagging down a plane. A taxi pulled over, and he shoved Serena into the backseat. Then he jumped in behind her and slammed the door. The photographer pressed his camera close to the window and Serena buried her face in Thaddeus's broad shoulder, feeling a little like Princess Di must have just before she died.

"Let's go, let's go!" Thad barked at the driver.

As they sped away, the photographer called after them. "That'll be the cover of the *Post* tomorrow!"

When they reached Seventy-first and Third, Thaddeus paid the driver and hopped out so he could open her door. Their footfalls echoed into the night, and the distant traffic on Second Avenue sounded vaguely like the ocean. Serena climbed the bottom step of her stoop and then turned. Standing there, she was at eye level with Thaddeus.

"Would you like to come up for a drink?" she asked, determined that the ugly incident with the paparazzi wouldn't put a damper on the evening. After all, this was the first time she'd had Thaddeus all to herself. There was no angry director, no fussy cinematographer, no script to follow. She wasn't going to let this moment pass.

He shrugged. "Maybe we should just sit here for a while." He sank down onto the stoop. "Are you okay?"

"I'm fine," she breathed, delicately pulling at her dress before sitting down next to him.

"That fucking photographer," he growled sulkily.

Serena put a protective hand on his leg. "He was just an asshole." She smiled cheerfully at him. "Don't worry about it. Come up and I'll make you a nice cold mojito."

"Sometimes I just get tired of it—the way they talk to you like they know you. The way he called me Thad, you know?" Thaddeus went on, ignoring her invitation. Serena blinked at the sliver of moon hovering over a Seventy-second Street highrise.

"It must be hard for you. I mean, people probably think they know you. They see your movies, they see you in magazines."

But they don't get to enjoy intimate dinners with him, poor babies.

"I mean, my name's not even Thaddeus, for Christ's sake."

"What do you mean?" she asked, confused.

"It's Tim. My agent thought it should be something catchier."

"I guess it worked." Serena nodded, wondering suddenly if she shouldn't change *her* name. It might be good for her career.

Yeah, Serena van der Woodsen isn't catchy at all.

He dug into his pocket and pulled out a soft pack of Parliament Lights. "At least it's quiet here," he said, lighting up.

That's right. You're safe, right here, with me. "No photographers here," Serena giggled. "Just the two of us."

"Working on our chemistry," Thaddeus laughed. "Our homework. Chemistry homework, get it?"

Better stick to the script, dude.

It was easily the best homework assignment Serena had ever been given, and she was sure she was acing it. The question was how to nuzzle up to him but make it clear she wasn't rehearsing. She wanted to make sure he saw her as Serena and not Holly, and that he could distinguish the fake kisses from the real thing.

"Hello, again," came a voice from above them. It was Jason, her downstairs neighbor, wearing a navy pinstripe suit. His blue-and-yellow-striped tie was loose around his neck and the collar of his white oxford shirt was unbuttoned. She hadn't seen him since he'd come to her rescue her first day in the apartment, and she'd actually sort of forgotten about him.

"Hi, Jason." Serena wanted to be polite but she honestly hoped he'd just disappear. He was friendly and cute but she and Thaddeus had homework to do.

"What's up?" Thaddeus put on that same, friendly, flirty tone he used on the talk show circuit. He extended a hand to Jason but remained perched on the stoop. "I'm Thaddeus."

Jason came down the steps. "I was just getting my mail. Hey, I'm Jason." He gave Thaddeus's hand a firm shake. "Nice to meet you."

"Pull up a step," Thaddeus joked, scooting over a little. "There's plenty of room."

"Or we could go upstairs to my place and get a drink," Serena suggested hopefully.

"Why don't I just grab some beers?" Jason offered. "I've got some inside. Then we don't have to bother with all those stairs."

"Excellent. I kind of like it right here. Nice breeze. Good company." Thaddeus grinned at Serena.

"Me too." She smiled back, even though she'd much rather have been upstairs and alone with him. If he wanted a breeze, she could always open a window.

Jason lived on the parlor floor, so it only took him a minute to dash inside and fetch three cold bottles of Heineken.

"Thanks." Thaddeus sighed as he cracked the top and tossed the cap onto the next step.

"Long day?" asked Jason.

"Seriously," Thaddeus agreed. "What do you do?"

"I'm a summer associate at Lowell, Bonderoff, Foster and Wallace," Jason explained before taking a long swig. A car honked loudly in the street. Serena looked at her watch. This conversation was really quite riveting, but frankly, she'd rather be soaking in a Bliss salt-and-sage bubble bath.

"They're my lawyers!" Thaddeus exclaimed excitedly, like Jason was the most interesting guy he'd ever met. "You don't know Sam, do you?"

"I know *of* him," Jason replied. "He's a partner over in the LA office, right?"

A gentle breeze lifted Thaddeus's messy hair off his forehead. "He's a real pit bull. God, I remember one time I was having this contract dispute with a studio and—"

"It's a small world." Serena yawned and pointed her ballet-slippered toes.

"Here's to a small world." Thaddeus lifted his bottle and clinked it against Jason's and then Serena's.

She chugged the entire contents of her beer and inched a little closer to Thaddeus. Even if their conversation was deathly boring, she knew she was in the presence of two sweet young gentlemen who would probably carry her up four flights of stairs to her apartment if she happened to drink too much and couldn't walk.

After all, she's always depended on the kindness of strangers.

the runaway bride

Blair Waldorf burst into the lobby of Claridge's like a woman on a mission, which was exactly what she was. She had to get back to her suite and sift through the packages she'd had delivered. She was particularly interested in revisiting the show-stopping wedding gown that had been her week's biggest quarry: at ten thousand pounds it was a splurge, even for her, but it was so perfect that it was worth every penny, and Blair knew her mother would agree. And if she didn't, Blair knew her father, Harold J. Waldorf, would: he was a fabulous gay man living the high life in the south of France. If anyone understood the thrill of finding the perfect wedding dress, he would.

She'd been meaning to schedule a weekend rendezvous with her dear old dad in Paris—surely it was time for Marcus to meet her parents? It was only a couple of hours away by the Chunnel, and it would be *so fun* to take a romantic train ride with her boyfriend and leave cousin Camilla behind. As she marched through the lobby, she spied the concierge standing behind her neat little desk. *Perfect,* Blair thought. She could have *her* make the arrangements! Blair stormed across the marble tiles to where the woman stood, scribbling notes in some sort of leather-bound ledger.

"I need some assistance," Blair ordered. "Tickets to Paris."

"Madam! Ms. er, Beaton-Rhodes?" asked the concierge, a

short, prim Asian woman sporting circular John Lennon–type glasses and a no-nonsense bob.

"It's *Miss Waldorf,* actually," Blair corrected her.

Not Mrs. *yet.*

"Yes, of course," the concierge apologized. "Madam, I'm just confirming your reservation for another week. Is that accurate?"

"Sure, sure." Blair waved her hand. She had business to attend to. "Like I was saying, I want to go to Paris. Like, immediately."

"That's fine, then. I'll just need a credit card. For the room charge."

"Can you just bill Lord Marcus?" Blair asked, irritated. "He's handling the whole thing."

"I see," nodded the concierge, making a note in her little leather notebook. "And will his Lordship be visiting soon? We'll need him to sign."

"I'm not sure," admitted Blair. She was on her way to set up the perfect romantic evening—lingerie, champagne, the whole thing—but technically she hadn't spoken to him all day, so he didn't even know that they had a date.

"Well, I'm afraid we're going to need to schedule a time for his Lordship to drop by and sign the papers," the concierge replied firmly.

"Fine," snapped Blair. "I'll figure out a time."

A group of Italian tourists meandered by, randomly snapping pictures of Blair while she fumed.

"Well, Miss . . ."

"Waldorf," she repeated.

"Miss Waldorf, we'll need to have that signature on the bill by tomorrow, or I'm afraid we're going to have to release the suite. We *do* have an interested party."

"Fine," Blair replied icily. "I'll call him right now." Blair dug out her telephone and selected the only number in her speed dial. Lord Marcus's phone rang and, as she could have predicted, there was no answer. She opted not to leave a message. She'd already left three that day. She didn't want him to think she was insane.

Like buying a wedding dress is sane?

"He's not answering," Blair informed the concierge. "He's very busy at work right now, but I'm sure I'll hear from him tonight. I'll arrange for him to come by and settle the whole matter, okay?"

It had only been a few days, but Blair had already lapsed into a Madonna-like English accent, clipping certain consonants and using phrases like "the whole matter."

"That's fine." The concierge nodded. "Just do remember that he'll have to sign the bill by tomorrow or we'll be obliged to release the room. I do hope he'll find a moment to get away from his wife and come by."

"Excuse me?" Blair demanded.

"I'm sorry?" the concierge replied snottily.

"What. Did. You. Say?" Blair could feel the tips of her ears glowing red with fury. For a moment she forgot about the dress waiting for her upstairs in her luxurious suite. She forgot about the maid, who would happily mix Blair whatever drink she requested as soon as she walked in. She forgot about the in-room massage she'd been itching for. She forgot about Paris.

"I believe I said, I hope he'll find a moment to get away from his life and come by," the concierge answered sweetly.

"You did not," Blair whispered tightly, leaning across the counter, her voice very quiet. "You said *wife*."

"I'm sure you misunderstood," the concierge replied.

"Well, I'm sure *you* misunderstood!" Blair shouted. She had never been shy. "I heard what you said."

"Yes, ma'am. Of course. I'll just need to have his Lordship pop by to sign the papers and the matter will be settled."

"He's not married. She's his *cousin*," Blair went on. "And I'm his girlfriend." She was practically shouting. On the other side of the lobby the Italians turned to look.

The concierge blushed deeply. "If we can just keep our voices down."

"Fuck that." Blair had had it with England, with everyone's polite prattle, with the British insistence on quiet dignity. Blair wasn't interested in quiet or in dignity. Fuck this bitch, fuck Britain, fuck Lord Marcus and fuck his horsey cousin Camilla. She suddenly wanted nothing more than to be home. "You know what? I don't want the room. I want you to call British fucking Airways and book me a ticket immediately. One way, first class. To New York." Blair dug into her bag and found her black American Express card, which she tossed onto the desk angrily.

"One way to New York, first class," repeated the concierge. "Virgin has flights at eleven daily. I'll see if we can get you a seat."

Virgin. How appropriate. Not.

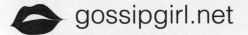
Disclaimer: All the real names of places, people, and events have been altered or abbreviated to protect the innocent. Namely, me.

hey people!

I'm sure some of you have seen it, and I bet you couldn't believe it any more than I could. There I was, happily traipsing down Madison Avenue, in search of some new washed-cotton beach cover-ups when what do I see? The worst sign ever: Closed. Closed? It's not what you think though: it seems that Barneys' creative director and dandy-about-town, Graham Oliver, is besties with a certain fashion-inept indie auteur and agreed to close up shop for a few days so the cameras can roll.

I just hope they reopen on schedule: the word is a certain starlet's debut performance might need a bit of tweaking. Things are so grim, in fact, they're shooting every scene she doesn't appear in first, in hopes that all her practice finally makes perfect.

Now that Barneys is closed for a while, I'm thinking of leaving town for good—no more of this popping back and forth on charter jets and helicopters. I know I said that things don't get cooking in the Hamptons for a while, yet—I usually wait until the Fourth of July to hunker down for the season—but I've been getting reports about some intriguing activity out on the Island. I might have to check it out myself. It's so hard to be me: how can I be in two places—or three or four or five—at once? Not that I've ever had a problem with it before.

summer survival guide

I'm not going to name names—unusual for me, I know—but there are plenty of repeat offenders out there. So as a refresher course, here's everything you need to know about:

1) Tanning

Obviously, the real thing is best. If Mother Nature isn't comply-ing, airbrushing is acceptable, but remember, whether poolside or in that little spray chamber, you must go naked: tan lines are a turn-off. And remember to wax two days before and exfoliate! Your streaks and splotches aren't fooling anyone.

2) Brows

For starters, you know you're supposed to have two, right? Now put down the tweezers. No, throw them away. Go see my friend Reese at Bergdorf's ASAP. And I don't want to hear any com-plaining about how it's $45 per brow.

3) Waxing

It's bathing suit season, so landscaping isn't optional. If you're going to be wearing that Eres bikini, we're all going to get a show. Personally, I endorse the traditional Brazilian (no pain, no gain). And while I've been known to opt for a precious little Swarovski crystal appliqué tattoo, there really is no need to gild the lily, is there?

your e-mail

Dear GG,
I heard there's a pretty racy film making the rounds on the Internet, and it proves that a certain someone has been in a movie before. It was shot on location in Central Park, with that stud N. Her hair looks kind of brown and curly, but it's got to be S, right?
—Cineaste

Dear Cineaste,
You're going to have to get your facts straight: there was a movie, from, like, a year ago, and no one involved in that

production has anything to do with what's filming here right now. That well-endowed star is off making art—and who knows what else—in Prague. Au revoir!
—GG

Dear GG,

There's this really annoying girl in my yoga class—I'm just trying to get in shape and keep busy while my best friend is at, like, art camp in Prague for the summer—but she's always going on about how yoga is a "way of life." Anyway, after class the other day she was gushing to the teacher about some new "spiritual book lover," crush and he sounded suspiciously like someone I know—only not. Like his evil twin. Or his good twin. Anyway, I'm confused. Are there pod people in town replacing everyone with clones or what?
—Scared

Dear Scared,

This is an intriguing development. I doubt it's aliens, though—sometimes it's nice to just enjoy a little summer fantasy. Haven't you ever pretended to be someone you weren't on vacation? Try it sometime: check into your hotel as the Principessa de Medici or something like that, and don't be surprised if management sends up an enormous fruit basket or some Dom Perignon. Stretching the truth sometimes has its merits.
—GG

sightings

B paying an excess-baggage fee at the Virgin counter at Heathrow. Souvenirs for friends and loved ones, or was it that oversize wedding dress garment bag? **N** picking up a few staples, like Visine and condoms, at White's Pharmacy in East Hampton. **D** enjoying a very healthy four-veggie smoothie at

Soho Natural. Maybe he's shaping up for swimsuit season? **S** might want to take a page from his book—after sneaking out of rehearsal early, she headed straight to the Tuleh sample sale near F.I.T. and then made a not-so-brief pit stop at Cold Stone Creamery. Now, now: looking like a star is half the work! Not that she ever has to worry.

You know you love me.

gossip girl

a little bird told me. . . .

"Nate Archibald. I can't believe my eyes."

"Hey, Chuck," muttered Nate. On his way home that afternoon, he'd noticed his front tire was a little low on air, so he'd pulled into the BP station on Springs Road. It had been an incredibly hot day, the kind of day with no ocean breeze to break up the haze, so Nate's hours of backbreaking labor had left him sweaty, sunburned, and exhausted. Judging from the horrified look on Chuck Bass's smooth, naturally tanned face, Nate figured he must look pretty terrible.

That's a first.

"What *happened* to you?" gasped Chuck. He pulled his vintage Ray-Ban aviators down the length of his nose and handed the gas station attendant a fifty-dollar bill. "Keep the change."

"Nothing happened, man," Nate responded, annoyed. He removed the hose from his tire and bounced the bike up and down to check the pressure.

Despite the thick heat, Chuck Bass was wearing madras board shorts and a gray cashmere hoodie. He looked as perfectly primped as usual, his thick eyebrows arched tidily above his piercing brown eyes, his aftershave-commercial-handsome square chin shaved smooth. He extended a hand to help Nate to his feet.

"Given up on cars?" Chuck asked, nodding at Nate's bike. "Don't tell me you've gone green on us."

"Yeah." Nate looked hopefully toward the tastefully gray-shingled BP gas station for someone to save him from Chuck.

"Let me give you a ride." Chuck rattled the ice in the plastic cup of chilled mocha latte that he'd drained. "It's a hundred degrees out and you look like you've been through hell. I don't want to imagine how you'll look after riding all the way back to Georgica Pond on that bike."

Nate weighed his options: half an hour sweating versus ten minutes alone with Chuck Bass?

Damned if you do, damned if you don't.

"Let's go." Nate sighed. The thought of Chuck's air-conditioned dove gray Jag was too hard to resist.

Chuck unlocked the car's trunk and Nate stuffed the bike into it—he wasn't sure it would fit, but the trunk was surprisingly big and they were able to rig it so only the tip of the tire poked through. Nate slid onto the white leather seat and slammed the heavy door, fastening his seat belt and gearing up for the ride.

Chuck turned on the ignition and the car immediately flooded with cold air and blared Zeppelin's "Houses of the Holy."

"I've been lying on the beach in Sag Harbor all day, feeling retro," Chuck explained, turning the volume down. "So . . . let's catch up."

"Catch up," echoed Nate blankly. He could tell from Chuck's tone of voice that he was going to launch into a barrage of questions. Talking with Chuck was like having a job interview.

"I assume you heard about Blair." Chuck fiddled with the air conditioner, even though it was already freezing. He pulled out onto the road connecting Hampton Bays to East Hampton, which Nate had practically memorized by now. Wine-grape fields alternated with tasteful Colonial-style, gray-shingled houses, and occasionally he caught a glimpse of the dark blue ocean behind someone's backyard.

"Blair?" Nate asked as they passed the Oyster Shack on the left. He'd been so preoccupied with Tawny, even saying Blair's name aloud felt weird. She was off in England for the summer with her new British boyfriend as far as he knew. She seemed far away when he thought about her, even though their paths would soon cross again. She might be madly in love with that new English dude, but there was no way Blair Waldorf was going to abandon her lifelong dream of going to Yale in the fall. A September reunion on campus was inevitable.

"She's *ba-a-a-a-a-ck*." Chuck drew it out like that creepy little girl in the movie *Poltergeist*. He rattled the ice in his cup and slurped up the coffee-flavored water that had gathered at the bottom. "Just got off the plane this morning."

"Oh yeah?" Nate fiddled with the shoulder strap on his seat belt. Blair was back from London? That *was* news.

"Yeah." Chuck nodded casually, turning the stereo down further. "I wonder if she and Serena have kissed and made up. *Again*. If you know what I mean."

"Blair and Serena never could stay mad at each other for long," Nate muttered, drumming his thumb against the door handle in time to the music. He would know—he usually caused the rifts between them.

"It's good news for Serena, though," Chuck added coyly. "She could really use a friend right about now."

Nate didn't respond. Everything Chuck said made him feel a little uneasy, like the world was moving on without him. He'd only been in the Hamptons for a week, and already he didn't know what the fuck was happening.

"Word is she's having a *little* trouble with the whole acting thing," Chuck observed. "But I'm sure she'll come out on top. She always does."

"Acting, right," Nate repeated. He'd forgotten about Serena's movie. It seemed totally alien from his life as a day laborer. Nate was suddenly overwhelmed with the desire for a smoke. He shoved in the car's electric lighter. "You don't mind, do you?"

Chuck shrugged. "No matter how much trouble Serena might be having, it's nothing compared to the mess Blair's got herself into." He drove fast, veered right at a fork, and caused the tires to squeal. The houses were getting grander and the lawns bigger the farther they drove.

"What trouble?" Nate demanded, igniting the half-smoked joint he'd wisely saved for just such a moment.

"Blair just came back from London in a hurry. With some . . . *parcels*."

"What parcels?" Nate already felt extremely stoned. Was it him, or was Chuck such a huge asshole he was almost not human, like an android or something.

"Well, when she was in London, Blair bought a bunch of things she just couldn't live without. Like a wedding dress. And one of those old-fashioned English baby carriages. Then she booked a ticket back to New York."

"What are you trying to say?" Nate demanded. A big white event tent set up on a lawn caught his eye. A frou-frou bride and mangy-haired groom holding a guitar were posing for pictures by an old oak tree not far from it. Wannabe rock star types were always getting married in the Hamptons.

"Blair's back in a big hurry, packing a wedding dress and a baby carriage. . . . I don't know." Chuck sighed impatiently. "You do the math."

That math wasn't hard—even for a stoner.

It would definitely take a major event to convince Blair Waldorf to cut her trip short. Had she come home to plan her wedding? Nate wouldn't put it past her, but he just couldn't imagine Blair putting on a wedding dress and marching down the aisle unless he was there, too, in a tuxedo, right by her side. Of course they weren't even together anymore, but somehow it was impossible for Nate to imagine Blair—*his* Blair— marrying anyone but him.

Nate was beyond relieved when they pulled into the

winding gravel driveway of the Archibald estate. He needed to be alone with this news and another, much larger joint.

"Thanks for the ride, man," Nate muttered distractedly, fumbling with his roach as he climbed out of the car.

"If you want to talk some more, Nate," Chuck called through the passenger window, "I can come in. We could order sushi."

Ignoring Chuck's pathetic, lonely offer, Nate retrieved his bike from the trunk and trudged up the driveway. He needed to clear his head.

He also needs to learn not to believe everything he hears. (Not that we don't all make that mistake from time to time.)

s follows in audrey's footsteps. literally.

Serena stepped out of a flaming yellow taxi onto a crowded stretch of Fifth Avenue, wearing a simple black shift and a pair of enormous sunglasses, courtesy of the designer Bailey Winter. She was in costume—even Serena wouldn't prance around the city in the middle of the day in a cocktail dress—rehearsing the opening scene of the movie. Holly had to peer into the display windows of the famous jewelry store Tiffany and Company while eating breakfast after a long night out, just like Audrey Hepburn did in the original movie.

Gripping a takeout cup of coffee and brown paper bag full of pastries provided by the prop department, Serena strolled primly toward the elegant building, counting the steps to herself, slowly and deliberately. *One, two, three, four.*

"Watch it," barked a suited businessman, brushing by her as he snarled into a cell phone.

"Sorry," Serena mumbled, feeling flustered. She walked back to the curb, turned around, and retraced her steps. She tried to keep her back perfectly straight, the way Ken had instructed her to, but she had to focus on making a direct path to the store, too, which was nearly impossible because there were so many people around. She finally made it, but the windows were completely blocked out by tourists, frantically snapping pictures of the window displays. That was definitely *not* in the script.

A chubby older woman in a tennis skirt held her camera out to Serena, gesturing that she wanted Serena to take her photograph. Serena shrugged, dropped the paper bag onto the street, and took the camera. She focused and took a picture of the woman, smiling and pointing to the Tiffany logo.

"Thanks! And now may I take a picture of you? You work for the store, right?" Serena was flabbergasted. Of course she must look like some moronic walking window display, hired by Tiffany in hopes that the nod to the old film would sell more jewelry. She kept a smile plastered to her face while the woman snapped away, then picked up her paper bag and walked back to the curb. A bus roared past, sending a blast of hot exhaust up her dress.

Aaah, summer in the city.

Serena looked up at the store, her whole body trembling with frustration. It was nearly a hundred degrees, she was sweating and overdressed, people were staring, and she just wanted to go home—to her parents' penthouse, not her cat-piss-scented dump—and change into linen boxers, a wifebeater, and some comfy flip-flops, and spend the afternoon drinking Coronas and watching a *Laguna Beach* marathon. She'd always managed to excel at everything, from school to horseback riding to boys, all without even trying. She'd been sure acting would come as easily to her as everything else she'd tried in her life, but so far Ken Mogul was clearly unhappy with her performance.

She wondered if even Blair Waldorf, the world's most diehard *Breakfast at Tiffany's* fan, would have been able to put up with Ken Mogul's maniacal tirades.

She started her approach toward Tiffany's once more.

"Look, sweetheart," a stocky, loud-voiced Southern woman cried, pointing out Serena to her balding, paunchy husband, who was sporting a winning ensemble of pleated khaki shorts and a knockoff Lacoste polo, topped off with black socks under his cheap leather mandals.

"Well, now I've seen everything," the man exclaimed.

"It's just like *Breakfast at Tiffany's*, isn't it?" the woman continued, approaching Serena. "Yoo-hoo, dear, is this some kind of publicity stunt?"

Serena pretended not to hear. Who knew Manhattan's sidewalks were so treacherous? She retreated back to the curb and steeled herself, then made the walk again.

Now that's dedication.

She might have looked like a funny tourist attraction to the people walking by, but inside she was a seething, frustrated actress on the verge of a major temper tantrum. The truth was, Serena didn't even want to act anymore; she wanted to give up and walk over to Barneys and see if anything new was on the racks. But of course she couldn't do that: first, because it was closed due to filming, so she was partly responsible for her own worst nightmare, and second, because she had never really failed at anything before and was secretly every bit as competitive as her sometimes best friend, Blair.

"Nice ass, blondie," called a deep voice from behind her.

Serena turned to see a guy leering at her from the backseat of a passing taxi. Gross. Audrey Hepburn never had to deal with this sort of crap.

No, but then again, Audrey Hepburn's ass was kind of flat. But at least she could act.

money isn't funny, honey

Blair couldn't tell if the pounding was in her head—she'd put away quite a few whiskeys on the plane—or if it was real. She lifted her head: no, it was real, and it was coming from the door to the bedroom where she'd crashed last night, the room formerly occupied by her hippie stepbrother, Aaron Rose.

"Blair Cornelia Waldorf!"

There was more pounding. It was her mother and her voice sounded . . . different. Was she sick? Did she have something in her mouth?

Eleanor Rose pushed the door open and stomped into the dark bedroom, perching on the edge of the mattress. She was carrying a mug of coffee and was dressed in her summertime sleep outfit, a flouncy, way-too-short peachy Eberjey slip and matching robe.

"Wake up!" she shrieked hoarsely.

Blair pulled the covers over her head and moaned. Why was her mother carrying on like this so early in the morning?

"Blair Waldorf," her mom hissed. "I'm serious, young lady. Come out from under there. We need to have a little chat."

"I hope you know I barely slept," Blair snapped, sitting up and snatching the coffee from her mother's hands. She took a long sip and tugged at the flimsy white Hanro camisole she'd chosen to sleep in.

"First," Eleanor ranted, "what are you doing home?"

Gripping her robe with one hand, she leaned in and studied her daughter's face. "You're supposed to be in London!"

For a fiftysomething-year-old who'd just had a baby, Eleanor looked pretty good in the morning. Blair wondered if her mom had had something done to her face while she was away, or maybe it was some new eye cream Blair would eventually steal.

"Something came up." Blair reached for the green-tea-soaked eyepads she kept in a drawer in her bedside table, placing one over each eye.

"Well, next time you might think to give me a call and let me know what you're up to." Eleanor snatched the eye pads away. "I had a call this morning from American Express. I don't like it when my credit card company knows my daughter's whereabouts before I do."

"What?" Blair demanded, sitting up a little straighter.

"American Express called because someone charged a $4,000 plane ticket to my account," Eleanor scolded. "I was about to call the police. Then I noticed the new blue leather Hermès luggage set in the foyer."

"I came in late," Blair explained. "I didn't want to wake you."

"That's only part of the problem." Eleanor stood and paced around the room. "Blair, it's about time you learned some responsibility. You're not a child anymore. You're going to *have* to learn how to manage your money."

This from the woman who bought each of her children a private island in the South Pacific!

"Mom," Blair whined.

"Don't 'Mom' me," Eleanor ordered sharply. "You know I never say no to my children, you know that, don't you? I've always given you whatever you wanted, haven't I?"

Well, wasn't that her job?

"Yes, I have." Eleanor had never given a parental lecture before, and Blair could see she was getting into it. "But this is too much. I talked it over with Cyrus and we agreed that something has to be done."

Excuse me, why was her mother discussing her private business with Cyrus Rose, her stupid, red-faced, tacky-assed stepfather? "I don't even know what you're talking about." Blair yawned, draining the coffee cup. She wondered how long this particular chat was going to last. The whole thing was just so . . . *boring*. She needed more sleep, and a long bath, and a facial to get rid of all the London grime, and maybe a haircut and a few face-framing highlights to go with her cleansed and exfoliated face.

"What I'm talking about, Blair, is this American Express bill." Eleanor shook a wrinkled fax. "I had them send it over as soon as the woman on the phone told me about your . . . shopping exploits."

Oops.

"Well, Mom," Blair admitted, "I might have gone a *little* overboard on the wedding dress, but once you see it, I know you'll agree—"

"*Wedding dress?*" her mother gasped. "I guess that explains the eighteen-thousand-dollar charge. What is this about a wedding?" She sat down on the bed and fanned herself with her diamond-encrusted fingers. "I feel like I'm going to faint! You're getting married? Oh, Blair! I don't know what to say!" She threw her arms around Blair and burst into noisy tears. Then she abruptly sat up. "No, wait, I do: over my dead damn body you're getting married! Have you lost your mind?!"

Blair rolled her eyes. "No, Mom, I'm not getting married. At least, not right away. Anyway, that dress was only ten thousand, not eighteen."

Oh, yes, that's much better.

"No, my dear, innocent child." Eleanor shook her head. "Didn't you realize that the exchange rate is almost two to one?"

"Look," Blair declared hurriedly, "I'm sorry, okay? I only bought a few things, and they're all for school."

Yeah. We all wear wedding gowns to freshman orientation.

It didn't look like she was going to escape any time soon. Blair picked up the new issue of *W* she'd left on the night table. She'd bought the oversize magazine to keep her occupied on the long flight, but the complimentary Maker's Mark bourbon had ended up being a much more interesting diversion.

"Blair." Eleanor sighed and squeezed Blair's knee through the purplish-brown hemp-blend bedspread. "I don't mind you buying a few things—but a wedding dress?" She paused. "Still, I bet it's quite a dress."

"It is!" Blair exclaimed. *This* was the mother she knew and sort of loved.

"Even so, I've talked it over with Cyrus, and I'm going to call your father this afternoon, but I think he'll agree that, since you're home now, presumably to stay—"

"I'm definitely *not* going back to London," Blair interjected, trying not to feel emotional about her dramatic departure from Marcus's hometown. Had he even noticed she was gone?

"—this is the perfect opportunity for you to find some work for the summer. A job."

A *what*? No comprende, señora.

The room was spinning. "What did you just say, Mom? A *job*?"

"Yes, dear. A job."

Blair fell back onto the pillows and threw her arm over her eyes. "But I'll *die* if I have to work."

"Don't overreact," Eleanor insisted. "It'll be a terrific experience before starting school."

"Have *you* ever worked?" Blair demanded. She began to flip through the magazine angrily, almost tearing the pages as she turned them. She'd just fled a country, having been spurned by the love of her life. A lecture from her never-worked-a-day-in-her-life mother on the merits of employment and pulling herself up by her bootstraps was the absolute *last* thing she needed.

"That's beside the point," Eleanor replied evenly. "We're not talking about me, we're talking about you helping to pay some of these exorbitant bills. If you're going to spend this much, you're going to have to earn something."

Work for the summer? Blair closed her eyes—no one she knew was working during this, their last summer vacation ever. No one! Well, except for Nate, but that was a punishment. There was Serena, too, but that wasn't really a job—it was a dream come true.

Blair's eyes suddenly came to rest on the page in front of her. *Speak of the fucking devil.* There, smack-dab in the middle of Suzy's latest reports on all the society gossip, was a photograph of Serena van der Woodsen arm in arm with the designer Bailey Winter. Blair remembered when that photograph had been taken, at Winter's runway presentation the previous season. She and Serena had been seated in the front row—naturally—and when the designer had come out to take his final bow, he'd noticed Serena in the audience and pulled her up onto the runway with him.

Tuning out her mother's relentless drone, Blair scanned the page to see whether there was some news about Serena. And indeed there was: Suzy's column was all about how Bailey Winter had signed on with Ken Mogul to provide the costumes for Mogul's new film project, *Breakfast at Fred's.* It wasn't enough that Serena got to star in a movie with Thaddeus Smith; she also got to wear custom designs by one of the best living American designers?

"I just think it's a matter of responsibility, Blair," her mother declared. "You know, when you turn twenty-one you'll get access to your trust fund, and your father and Cyrus and I need to know that you'll handle the money responsibly. We feel very strongly that a job is the perfect way for you to learn to manage money and carry out other people's wishes, not just your own."

Blair glared at the ugly eggplant-colored bedspread. Fine, she'd get a summer job. But she was not going to settle for anything less than the most glamorous summer job imaginable.

"You know," she mused, "maybe you're right. Maybe a job is just what I need to keep myself busy this summer."

"Yes!" her mother cried happily. "I knew you'd come around!"

"And maybe you can help me get one?" Blair asked sweetly.

"Of course!" Eleanor agreed. "I'm sure we can make some phone calls and find you something wonderful in no time at all!"

There was, of course, only one telephone call she needed her mother to make. Being the daughter of Eleanor Rose, Bailey Winter's most loyal couture client, would surely come in handy when it came to landing an assistantship on the set of *Breakfast at Fred's.*

If you can't beat 'em, join 'em!

it's getting hot in here

Furtively cupping the butt in his palm, Dan took a long last drag on his cigarette and tossed it to the ground, stubbing it out quickly and exhaling smoke into the breeze. He was stationed on a bench at the corner of Sixth Avenue and Houston and could see Bree crossing the street. He didn't want her to catch him smoking—again.

"Dan!" Bree called out, dodging the battalion of cabs creeping up Sixth Avenue, waving excitedly. She was wearing short, stretchy black pants that flared a little at her calves and a turquoise sports bra and was carrying a gray Nalgene water bottle. She trotted through the traffic and up to the bench.

"Hi! It's so good to see you."

"You too," Dan replied, oh-so-casually closing his book and grinning at her.

"Oh! You're reading *The Way of the Artist!*" she exclaimed. "I *love* that book."

"Really?" Dan had a feeling she might. "That's a funny coincidence."

Sure it is.

"Totally," giggled Bree. "First *Siddhartha*, now *The Way of the Artist?* You must be the Strand's spiritual expert."

"Oh, definitely," Dan lied. "Everyone they hire has a different specialty."

"Cool." Bree grabbed his hand and yanked him up off the bench. "Now come on! We're going to be late."

"Okay," Dan agreed cheerfully. "I hate missing the previews."

"Previews?" Bree asked. "We're not going to the movies. Remember? We're going to Bikram."

"Uh, yeah," Dan replied nervously. *Bikram, Bikram, Bikram.* Not a movie. Maybe a restaurant? "Right. Um, good, I'm, uh, starving."

Bree laughed. "Yeah, I'm pretty hungry for some exercise myself. Let's hurry so we don't miss this class—the evening sessions are even more intense than the ones I usually take. And maybe afterwards I'll buy you a Jamba Juice."

Class? Jamba Juice? She might as well have been speaking Swahili. Dan had no idea where they were going but he followed Bree down the street, making idle chitchat about books he hadn't actually read and getting more and more worried. It didn't seem likely that they were going to a restaurant. Then Dan looked up and saw it, looming in the distance: a hand-painted sign with a funny, Indian-style font that was supposed to look like Sanskrit that proudly proclaimed BIKRAM. It wasn't a movie. It wasn't a restaurant. Bikram was a kind of *yoga*. Bree was taking him to a yoga class.

Namaste!

Bree trotted up the stairs eagerly, like a kid on Christmas morning. She turned and glanced over her shoulder at Dan, who was lagging behind, trying to think of an excuse not to participate. He decided to feign an injury and was trying to choose a part of his body he could claim to have hurt. He had a cracked rib maybe, from lifting too many dictionaries. He'd been hit by a car on his way to work this morning and was pretty sure he was concussed. He had a rare neural disorder that caused him to black out in small crowded rooms full of sweaty people lying on colorful rubber mats.

"PS, Dan," Bree called down to him. "I'm glad you didn't

bother with a change of clothes. For the evening sessions, Yogi keeps the heat even higher than usual, so we usually just go naked."

Now things were getting complicated. First, there was no way he was going to do yoga, and second, he'd be damned if he was going to do yoga *naked*. On the other hand, Bree would be there too; he'd get to see her completely naked the very first time they hung out.

"Um, great!" he enthused, already out of breath from climbing the stairs. Dan had never exercised in his life, but the sight of Bree's round, yoga-firm butt a few steps above him was all the motivation he needed. Forget that he'd never done yoga, never mind that he was sure to be humiliated, and fuck the seemingly endless flight of stairs: he was going to get into all sorts of pretzel-like positions with Bree, *naked*. What was there not to love?

That's the spirit!

"Come on!" Bree urged giddily.

Dan reached the top of the stairs and followed her into the Tranquility Yoga Studio, a wide-open space with gleaming wide-plank pine floors. The room was almost all windows and was flooded with the late afternoon sun—and the rays only intensified the heat. The temperature in the room must have been near a hundred and twenty degrees, and with the sunlight and all the naked bodies, it was also humid and very . . . *fragrant*.

On a platform in the front of the room was an emaciated-looking Indian man with gleaming, well-oiled skin, dressed only in a loosely cinched white cotton robe, seated with his spindly legs crossed in front of him. Below his thinly tweezed eyebrows his eyes were closed, and he was smiling beatifically. In front of him was a fortyish Katie Couric–looking woman doing her warm-up stretches, her paunchy tummy hanging loosely over her bare, veiny thighs.

A couple of guys warmed up by the windows—one with

long, sinewy muscles who arched his back in a way that just didn't look natural, and a silver-haired grandfather type touching his toes effortlessly. He really put Dan to shame . . . in every department.

"Better get undressed." Bree winked at Dan. "Master doesn't like to start class even a minute late. Anyone who's not undressed and ready to go is asked to leave."

Dan had been on the verge of explaining to Bree that he was epileptic and had forgotten to take his medication, but then she started to yank her turquoise sports bra over her head. Wow. What could he do?

Strip!

He pulled his dirty T-shirt over his head and let it fall to the ground. Then he unbuckled his belt, kicked off his shoes, and pulled down his jeans. He was the only guy in the room wearing boxer shorts, but he stubbornly kept them on.

Like his vampire tan and skinny arms didn't make him stand out enough.

He balled his socks up and stuffed them into his shoes, then took a deep breath and followed Bree out onto the floor, where she started to stretch. Her flawless skin was tan *all over*, which he knew for sure, since he could see *everything*. Her long blond hair fell over one of her handful-sized breasts and Dan had to remind himself he couldn't just go and grab them right now. She bent over and touched her palms to the floor. He tried to mimic her, but he could barely touch his knees. It was agonizing.

"Don't bend," Bree whispered. "Stretch, stretch."

It was impossible to see Bree's perfect naked body stretching and contorting without the fly of his boxers expanding to embarrassing proportions. Dan stared as she took her foot in her hand and extended it straight over her head. He closed his eyes and tried to think of unsexy things, like the way food always got stuck in his aunt Sophia's dentures or how the sidewalk in front of his building always smelled like dog piss. The sweat was already pouring down his face and they hadn't even done anything yet. He used his forearm to wipe the sweat from his brow.

"Dan, no!" whispered Bree. "Don't let master see you do that. The whole point is to sweat it out. You can't wipe it off. It goes against his teachings."

Why couldn't Bikram have been a nice foreign film? They could be eating popcorn in a dark, air-conditioned theater making out instead of sweating in this stifling room and following the orders of some sadist. Suddenly the teacher rose from his seated position on the dais at the front of the room and let his robe drop to the floor.

"Namaste!" he called, in a joyful, booming voice, bowing slightly.

"Namaste!" the rest of the class replied, bowing back.

Well, most of the class.

"Let's begin with partner poses." He motioned for everyone to pair up. "Prepare for shoulder stand. Begin with downward-facing dog and tripod pose, if you wish."

"Ready?" Bree whispered. She had a thumbnail-sized birthmark the shape of Texas near her belly button.

Bree bent over and placed her palms on the floor in front of her and then waggled her butt as if in preparation for take-off. Dan looked around, alarmed, but everyone else was doing the same thing. Their partners were even gently holding their hips. Dan tentatively touched Bree on the waist and she brought her right knee to her right elbow and then did the same with her left.

"Hold me steady," she told him. Dan crouched next to Bree, his hands circling her taut middle as she brought her long, toned legs straight up and smiled at him from upside-down. "I think I have it now."

"Oh, okay," Dan said, backing away. But as he went to stand up, he realized that his boxers were totally gaping in front and his "friend" was totally exposed . . . and totally excited. Oh, God. He stayed in a half-crouch, desperately trying to picture Aunt Sophia's cruddy teeth again.

"Young man." The scary naked yoga master pointed at Dan.

Me? Dan pointed at himself, still half-crouching. Everyone in the class turned to look at him.

"Yes, you. Come, my son," the teacher said, beckoning to Dan with his long, skinny fingers.

"Go up there," Bree whispered from upside-down. "This is such an honor, I can't believe it—on your first time, too."

Dan walked across the wooden floor trying to look casual, desperately cupping his crotch with his hands. He reached the foot of the platform and the teacher smiled down at him placidly.

"Come, my son," the teacher said. "You'll work with me today. It's your first time, right?"

Dan nodded nervously. His whole body trembled as he stepped onto the platform. The yogi reached down and placed his worn palms on the floor, giving Dan a terrible close up of his elephant-skin-wrinkled ass. Everyone in class followed suit, and for a brief second Dan got a surreal glimpse of Bree's bare breasts upside down from between her wide-spread legs. His reverie was interrupted as the teacher grabbed him from behind, pressing his bare stomach into Dan's skinny bare back, and gently guided his head down, so that all Dan could see were his own legs and the skinny legs of the naked guy straddling him. Dan had never been intimate with an older person before, let alone an old Indian yoga geezer.

But when a guy wants a girl, he has no shame.

n goes native

"I know a great place where we can go after this," Tawny announced. She licked her thumb and stuck it into the greasy basket of popcorn shrimp to pick up some fried crumbs.

Nate took a last swig from his limey Corona and nodded. "Fine by me."

Crammed into a tiny table by the Oyster Shack's greasy windows, they ate with their fingers, sipped beer, and talked— well, Tawny did most of the talking. About how she was learning to surf. About how her dad used to be a fire chief but had gotten hurt falling off a ladder and retired. About how she'd been to Disney World four times. About how her hair was naturally curly, but people always thought she had a perm. About how excited she was to finally graduate next year.

Nate barely listened to what she said: she was sexy as hell, and he enjoyed simply looking at her. There weren't many girls like Tawny on the Upper East Side: full, blond, wavy hair spilling over caramel, freckled shoulders, pink lips that tasted like cherry ChapStick, long-lashed bright blue eyes, and slender, tanned fingers covered with silver rings.

Blair was always quizzing him on his favorite song, his first memory, what he wanted to do when he grew up. She said she just wanted to get to know him, but it always felt like a test he was failing. Tawny seemed happy just to let Nate be who he was.

A hot, arrogant pothead?

When dinner was over, Tawny perched on the handlebars of his bike and shouted directions to Nate. She threw her head back and her long wavy hair tickled his nose.

"Slow down! No, speed up!" she shrieked.

"Where are you taking me?" Nate shouted as they bumped over tree roots and rocks.

Tawny glanced over her shoulder at him. "You'll see. . . . Hey, stop! Let me off."

Nate skidded to a stop and Tawny hopped onto the ground. Her lavender-colored hot pants had ridden up, giving him a great view of her tan, surf-toned ass cheeks. Shit, was she foxy! "That was fun," she laughed, crashing through some low bushes toward the beach. "Ditch the bike. It'll be safe there."

Nate leaned his bike against a nearby tree. The late afternoon sunlight filtered through the boughs overhead, but it was cool and very still in the woods.

Following Tawny, Nate thought about how weird it was that he'd only been out of school for a couple of weeks and yet his entire life had completely changed. He was working construction and dating a hot Hamptons chick. Well, why not? If Blair could change everything—she was getting married, for Christ's sake—why couldn't he? It was easier to be with Tawny than it was to be with any other girl he'd ever known; she wasn't demanding and self-absorbed like Blair, she wasn't naïve and needy like Jenny, she wasn't unpredictable and inattentive like Serena. She just . . . was.

Classic stoner logic.

"Come on," Tawny urged, backtracking to grab his hand and pull him through the bushes.

She led him into a sun-dappled clearing where two massive trees had fallen on top of one another, creating natural benches that were obviously popular with the locals, since the forest floor was littered with old beer bottles and cigarette butts. Three guys hunkered on one of the felled logs, passing a joint between them. Behind them, through the trees, the blue-black water of the sound glinted and swelled.

"Hey guys!" Tawny cried.

Three heads swiveled in their direction. With their baggy jeans and plucked eyebrows, gelled hair, and dorky striped button-downs, these were the kind of guys Nate and his friends would have scoffed at if they'd ever come across them in the city. They were the kind of guys who got into fights with bouncers and wore gallons of cheesy drug-store cologne. And they were also, apparently, Tawny's friends.

"Nate, these are Greg, Tony, and Vince."

"What's up?" Nate asked, nodding uneasily in their direction.

Tawny clambered over the trunk and took a seat next to Greg, a deeply tanned guy cupping a joint in his palm and jutting his chest out into the air territorially in a way that reminded Nate of a bulldog.

"We've got some herb, bro," announced Vince, who appeared to be Greg's twin. "Have a seat."

Nate's ears pricked up at this offer. He hated being called "bro" by guys he didn't even know, and he hated guys who pretended to be cool when they were really losers, but he had to admit a smoke—even with these dorks—sounded like his kind of dessert.

Tawny took a hit and handed over the slightly damp roach. Nate inhaled greedily.

"Good stuff, right?" the guy called Greg asked gruffly. "I got it off my regular guy. He's always busiest in the summer, you know, but he saves the best shit for loyal year-round customers like me."

It wasn't great stuff—the Hawaiian stash Nate had stored back in his bedroom was much better—but he couldn't complain.

"Fucking city kids," growled Vince, taking the joint from Nate. "They always fuck everything up during the summer. Fucking traffic. Fucking clubs. Fucking pain in the ass."

Eloquently put.

"Summer crowds, man," mumbled Tony, who hadn't yet spoken. He was glaring at Nate, studying him suspiciously from under the perfectly creased bill of his Coney Island Cyclones baseball cap.

Nate was zoning out as usual, the way he liked to when he was smoking herb, but he heard what the guys were saying. Loud and clear.

"Totally." Tawny yawned, lazily resting her blond, curly-haired head on Nate's shoulder.

Nate glanced down at his tattered work outfit. It was pretty clear Tawny disliked the wealthy crowd that flooded the Hamptons every summer, and Nate was definitely part of that crowd. With his workingman's tan and ragged clothes, she'd probably taken him for the kind of guy who had to spend his summer *earning* his money, presumably to pay his way through Yale in the fall. He felt a stab of guilt. He hadn't exactly been honest with her.

Old habits die hard.

"Same old story every year," Tony continued. "Why don't they find someplace else to go, like France or some shit?"

"They're not so bad," Nate ventured. "I mean, I'm kind of from the city—"

"You *are*?" Tawny demanded, lifting her head. She narrowed her normally wide blue eyes. "You never said anything."

"You never asked," Nate pointed out. There were murmurs from the other guys. Vince spat into the sand. Out on the water, a fishing boat flashed its lights.

"I knew it," Tony said, spitting on the ground. "I could just smell it on you."

"But I mean, it's no big deal." Nate shook his head. "I mean . . . I'm not like a lot of those kids."

"Well, I guess . . ." Tawny sank back into him, rubbing the side of her face against his work-strong chest. "Maybe you'll take me back to the city some time?"

"Sure, sure." Nate wrapped his tanned arm around her waist. "That'd be fun."

As long as he keeps her away from Blair Not-so-good-with-jealousy Waldorf.

come up and see me sometime

The evening after their study session and another disheartening day of rehearsal, Serena sat in the backseat of a taxi on her way back to the Chelsea Hotel. But this time, she had something to look forward to. She checked the text messages on her phone again, mostly because she wanted to reread the note from Thaddeus.

Come down and see me. I miss you. xx

Serena had been starting to doubt herself after all the insults from Ken Mogul, but here it was: incontrovertible, digital proof that she, Serena van der Woodsen, still had it.

The taxi made a wide turn onto Twenty-third Street and Serena felt her heart start to pound a little faster—in just a few minutes she'd be at the hotel. She'd been with handsome guys before, but she'd never fallen for anyone quite like Thaddeus. Of course he was gorgeous, but there was something else about him. Serena felt like they could be more than costars, more than lovers—they could be best friends, too.

Not that she needed a new best friend. Or did she? She could never remember.

When they reached the Chelsea at last, she stuffed a twenty-dollar bill into the driver's hand, burst from the backseat, and dashed into the lobby of the hotel. Even though filming had begun at Barneys, Ken had said she needed as much off-set practice as she could get. The familiar dark hallways lined with famous paintings gave Serena a sinking feeling in the pit of her stomach, but she tried to forget about all the negative things that Ken had yelled at her in the building and focus on what was about to happen: she was about to get together with Thaddeus Smith.

She knocked softly on his door and he pulled it open almost immediately, a startled look on his face. His very baggy cargo shorts had slid down to reveal his simple gray boxers.

"Serena," he exclaimed. "What's going on?"

"Nothing," she breathed, brushing past him and into the room. She tossed her khaki-colored Marc Jacobs drawstring beach bag on the floor and plopped onto the couch.

Thaddeus closed the door and pulled his shorts up, blushing slightly. "So," he said. "What's happening? Were you just in the neighborhood?"

"Something like that." Serena laughed. It was cute to see the world-famous actor squirming. God, she loved flirting with him.

"So," Thaddeus mumbled, picking up his discarded T-shirt from the floor and pulling it over his head. He sat in the armchair and placed his feet on the coffee table. "Have you been rehearsing on your own?"

"It's such a drag," Serena sighed. "But Ken acts like I'm never going to get it right."

"I always say it's harder work than people think," Thaddeus agreed. "People think it's all glamour, all parties and premieres, but I fucking *earn* my paychecks. I guess I don't need to tell you that."

Making three million per movie must be hard.

"I wish someone had warned me." Serena picked her bag up off the floor and dug her hand inside. She'd gotten so worked up on her way over, she needed to relax. "Mind if I smoke?"

"No, of course not." Thaddeus gestured lamely at the coffee table, which was already set with an ashtray and several lighters. "The thing is, Serena, this isn't a great time. My friend Serge is supposed to stop by."

Serena stayed where she was. Why was it so hard to get a minute alone with him?

"Well, your text message didn't sound like you were that busy." She smiled nervously. His coy act *was* a little confusing.

Only a little?

"Shit," Thaddeus exclaimed. "*You* got my text message?"

"Uh-huh," she murmured breathily.

"Well, I'm glad you did," he stammered. "I thought that we could, um, well, I thought that maybe we should get some work done."

Why was he so nervous? It was hard to believe that someone as gorgeous and successful as Thaddeus Smith could be so shy around girls! "*Work*." She pouted. "I thought you might want to, you know, have a little fun?"

"Fun," repeated Thaddeus. "Work can be—" His chirping cell phone interrupted him. He glanced at the display. "Serena, I've got to grab this. I'm sorry. I'll be just be a second." He scurried into the bedroom, so all Serena could hear was "Hello."

She stubbed out her half-smoked cigarette. Thaddeus's freaky behavior was starting to make her nervous. Was she coming on too strong? Not strong enough? He was the one who'd sent her a sexy text message. Why would he invite a friend over? Maybe Thaddeus was kinky? That wasn't really her thing.

Oh, really?

"Sorry about that," Thaddeus apologized, shuffling back into the room. He tossed his phone onto the coffee table, where it landed with a bang. "Anyway, as long as you're here, let's run some lines."

"Lines?" asked Serena.

"You can use my script," Thaddeus said, sinking into the armchair with a sigh. "I've got my lines down."

"Let's start with scene seventeen," she offered hopefully. "You know, the love scene?"

Rehearsing a love scene might be as close as she's going to get.

tea for two

"You okay?" Vanessa asked Dan. He was sprawled across his bed, wincing in pain. There were Camel butts all over the worn brown carpet, as if he couldn't be bothered to get up and get one of the half-empty coffee mugs he usually used as an ashtray.

"Fuuuuu-*uuuck*," he muttered. "I think I pulled something."

Vanessa picked up the dog-eared beige copy of the Bhagavad Gita from his unmade bed. She knew it was some sacred Indian text, but she'd never had any interest in finding out any more about it. Then she noticed Dan was working on a poem in his big black notebook. He rolled over onto his back.

"Whatcha writing?" she asked, reaching for the notebook. She read the first couple of lines:

Pure love. Pure lust. Trust trust.
Buddha was no Jesus. Neither am I.
I'm just a guy.

News flash: Bikram yoga kills creative brain cells, causing poets who already write bad poetry to write *really* bad poetry.

"You can't read that!" Dan snatched the notebook out of her hands. "It's, um, private."

"Do you want some tea?" he asked, sitting up. "I just bought some Mint Meltdown. It's supposed to empty the body of toxins and help your body really *breathe*."

Vanessa snorted. "You're joking, right?"

"Come on." Dan yawned. He rose to his feet unsteadily, and Vanessa followed him out of the bedroom and down the dark hall, moving at a grandfather's pace through the swinging door into the kitchen, which was filled with stacks of dirty dishes. There were breadcrumbs all over the counter and the toaster was lying on its side. Rufus had left a fondue pot filled with cheese in the middle of the butcher-block island. Vanessa took a fork and poked at its thick skin while Dan microwaved two mugs full of water.

Dan dropped two bags of Mint Meltdown into the mugs and handed her one. Vanessa tried to catch his eye, but weirdly, he wouldn't look at her. This was partly due to the fact that Vanessa looked pretty in her new black cap-sleeve dress and partly because he was wracked with guilt for getting sweaty with Bree and not even mentioning anything about it to his supposed girlfriend.

"So," she began tentatively. "I feel like I've hardly seen you."

"I've been working a lot," he replied, burying his nose in his mug. "They really need me at the Strand. And I've made some new friends."

Vanessa chuckled. "I guess the high-stakes world of used-book retail never quits." Why was he acting so bizarre? She'd been able to tell he was disappointed a couple days ago about her working such long hours, but ever since she moved in they'd been like *new* roommates who didn't even know each other.

"You don't have to be rude," Dan countered, tapping his spoon against the top of his BEAT POETS DO IT ON THE ROAD travel mug. "Judgment leads but to the path of negative energy."

"Excuse me?" Vanessa whispered shrilly. "Could you run that by me again?"

"I don't expect you to understand." He sipped his tea even

though it was still scalding hot. "It's one of the elemental sign-posts of the yogi's philosophy."

"The only yogi I know is the bear who steals the picnic baskets. I don't know where you picked up this New Age talk, but the Dan Humphrey I used to know and love and kind of had the hots for would think you are full of shit."

"Well, the Vanessa Abrams *I* used to know and love wouldn't be caught dead slaving for a Hollywood sellout," Dan retorted angrily. He left out the "kind of had the hots for" part since he kind of had the hots for someone else at the moment.

"Excuse me?" Vanessa set her cup down. Now that was just plain unfair. He *knew* Ruby had kicked her out and she needed the money. And wasn't he proud of her working on a feature film at the age of only eighteen? "At least my job requires more skill than alphabetizing dusty old books by author name."

He closed his eyes and breathed in noisily through his flared nostrils, something he'd learned yesterday in yoga. *In with the good, out with the bad.* "I thought living together would be so great, but I think you've changed."

Vanessa sighed over her steaming cup of tea. It tasted like Aquafresh toothpaste and Pine-Sol. "You're the one who's changed," she shot back. "Maybe I should just get out of your hair." She blew into her mug.

"Please," Dan retorted angrily. "You wanted *me* out of your hair, not the other way around. *I* was the one who cared about this summer together. *You* just wanted to work."

"Well, I guess we're both getting what we want." Vanessa took another sip of Mint Meltdown tea before setting it down on the counter among the old newspapers and food-encrusted saucepans. Then she stomped out of the kitchen and out of the apartment to get a decent cup of coffee at the greasy deli up on Broadway.

Dan ran his hands through his messy light brown hair. He was having a meltdown all right, but not the right kind of meltdown. He pulled a pack of Camels out of the pocket of his faded black cords and lit one using the front burner on the gas stove.

Surely Yogi would not approve.

imitation is the sincerest form of flattery

Blair slipped her feet into the ivory calfskin Winter by Bailey Winter stilettos she'd chosen as the finishing touch to her interview outfit. They were a tad over the top, maybe, but she had to wear something by the man himself. It would have been so cheesy to show up in his clothes, but shoes were a sly, subtle way to acknowledge his greatness without looking like some dorky, desperate fashion groupie.

Blair was in baby Yale's nursery—aka her former bedroom—admiring herself in the full-length mirrors—the light was so much better there than in Aaron's dingy room, where the stink of his herbal cigarettes was embedded in the walls. She nodded at herself in the mirror. She looked confident, but she felt nervous. Blair had a history of bad luck with interviews—she had actually *kissed* her interviewer when she was applying to Yale. Then, when she'd requested a second interview with a Yale alumnus, she'd almost *slept* with him. Chances were slim she'd end up making a pass at Bailey Winter—he was handsome enough in a super-tan, blinding-white-teeth kind of way, but Blair was definitely not his type.

Ahem. Not unless she changed her name to *Sir* Blair.

She turned and glanced over her shoulder to catch her reflection from a different angle. Getting this interview had been even easier than she'd hoped—all it had taken was a call from Eleanor Rose—but this was her big chance and she didn't want to blow it.

Serena could have her Hollywood stardom; Blair would have a career in fashion. She knew all the right designers, stores, and magazines: she really understood clothes and how to wear them. One day very soon she'd be a world-famous fashion muse. She'd sit in the front row at every Bailey Winter show, have a fragrance named after her, and appear in his ad campaigns. Their relationship would be just like Audrey Hepburn's relationship with the house of Givenchy—the stuff of legend. Let Serena play at being Audrey Hepburn onscreen: Blair would *be* Audrey Hepburn in real life.

But didn't Serena *already* have a perfume named after her? Oops.

The insistent chime of her Vertu cell phone echoed from Aaron's old room, interrupting her daydream. She'd been back in New York for forty-eight hours, but no one had called her, on either her U.K. line, which only Lord Marcus had the number to, or her regular phone, which was how the whole world reached her. She was living in exile, she told herself, and refused to rejoin society until she could make some dramatic statement—for example, that she'd flown back from the U.K. at Bailey Winter's special request. She couldn't have it leaking out that she was back because Lord Marcus was more interested in making googly eyes at his horse-faced cousin than in ravishing Blair in her huge hotel bed.

As if we don't have ways of finding out the truth.

She dashed back to Aaron's room and whisked the phone off the bureau. The display read MARCUS. His Lordship himself.

She pressed the receive button. "What?" she demanded rudely.

"Blair, darling, what happened? I've been trying to reach you."

"I don't really see what we have to talk about," Blair replied icily. "If you wanted to talk, you had plenty of time when we were still on the same *continent.*"

"You mean you've left?" Lord Marcus remarked, clearly surprised. "I thought maybe you'd just moved hotels or gone off to Paris to see your father or something. I was so worried."

"I'm sure you were," Blair snapped sarcastically, heading back toward Yale's room.

"This isn't about Camilla, is it, dearest? Because, you see, we're second cousins, so of course—"

"Of course *what?*" Blair demanded, watching her face flush in the full-length mirror. "To be honest, I'd rather not know, honestly. If you want to get all *Flowers in the Attic*, it's your business. Anyway, I don't have time for this—I'm a woman in demand. I'm a muse!"

"You're amused, love? It was all a misunderstanding then?" Lord Marcus responded happily. "Camilla is asking about you as well. She'll be so relieved."

"Send her my regards," Blair quipped. She pressed end, then slipped the battery out of the telephone's body and it went dead. After inspecting it closely to make sure there were no tiny parts that might come off, she left it in baby Yale's crib.

Because you're never too young for your first cell.

Blair glanced at her Chanel bracelet-watch. She was due at Bailey Winter's soon, and it wouldn't do to be late. She walked down the long hall toward the kitchen, where she found her mother stationed at the marble-topped island, nibbling on a cold rillette sandwich despite the fact that they were supposed to be leaving any minute. Blair's younger brother, Tyler, and his girlfriend, Jasmine, were clustered around her on low-backed stools, sipping Cokes.

"Nice to see you again, Blair." Jasmine beamed an adoring smile across the cool white kitchen.

Jasmine was Blair's stalker. This had become infinitely clear when she showed up at Blair's graduation party wearing the exact same white Oscar de la Renta suit Blair was wearing. Her nearly-black hair was remarkably shiny and healthy looking, but she was probably the most annoying person alive.

"Mom," Blair ordered, ignoring Jasmine. "Put that down. We've got to get going."

"Hush," her mother reprimanded, dusting some invisible crumbs off the marble-topped island. "We've got time. Besides, I've been going to Bailey Winter's house for years. That man is always ten minutes late. It's a known fact." She took another bite of her sandwich.

"Bailey Winter?" Jasmine looked excited. She spied Blair's shoes. "*Those* are Bailey Winter! I have the same ones in black. I should've gotten the ivory."

Blair glared at her.

"Hey Blair?" asked Tyler as he simultaneously downloaded songs onto his iPod and sent a text message. His eyes kept darting from one screen to the next.

"Yes?" She tapped her stilettoed foot impatiently. Could they please just get the fuck out of here?

"Did you really go all the way to London and not bring me, like, even one present?"

"Sorry," she sighed. "I came back in kind of a hurry."

"Although you certainly found time to buy yourself a few things," Eleanor observed, popping a picholine olive between her lips.

"I'm Jasmine." Tyler's girlfriend hopped to her feet and extended her hand to Blair. "You're Blair, of course. We actually met before, but you were hosting your graduation party, so you may not remember."

As if Blair could possibly forget her little imitator.

There was something suspicious about a thirteen-year-old with such good manners. In fact, there was something suspicious about Tyler having a girlfriend—he'd never seemed even remotely interested in girls before, preferring instead the company of his computer, his hookah, and his vinyl record collection.

"Let's go, Mom," Blair demanded. "I don't want to be late. This is my chance to make a really great impression."

"Oh, honey." Eleanor finished her sandwich and tossed the remains on the counter for Myrtle to clean up. "I'm so glad to see you taking this so seriously."

"Wait, are you going to *see* Bailey Winter?" Jasmine demanded.

Wouldn't she like to know.

"He's interested in hiring me," Blair informed her icily.

"I just *love* his clothes," Jasmine gushed. "Of course, I'm not supposed to buy anything that's not B by Bailey Winter— my mom says I have to wait until I start high school before I'm allowed to get my hands on the good stuff, but that's okay by me. I mean, I have to wear a uniform anyway, so—"

"Yeah, whatever." Blair cut her off. Did she *ask* for this kid's life story? "I'm going down to ask the doorman to hail a cab. Mom, you better be ready in five minutes or I'm going without you."

Blair rode down to the lobby alone and stood in front of the building smoking and keeping time on her Chanel watch. After precisely five minutes had passed, Eleanor breezed out of the building in a grapefruit-colored Bailey Winter shirtwaist dress and beige Tod's flats. But she wasn't alone: Jasmine was scurrying excitedly next to her like a three-year-old before her first *Nutcracker* performance. Blair was unfazed. There was a movie playing in her head: the waifish muse was on her way to visit her genius couturier. Even Jasmine couldn't fuck it up.

When they reached Bailey Winter's grand Beaux Arts mansion on Park Avenue, Blair was first out of the car. Her mother and Jasmine followed behind like ladies-in-waiting. When it came time to edit her little film, the bit players could easily be removed.

They were greeted at the door by an honest-to-God English butler, in a morning suit and everything, who announced them by name after he led them to the second-floor parlor: "Miss Eleanor Rose, Miss Blair Waldorf, and Miss Jasmine James-Morgan," he cried in his booming voice. It reminded Blair of Lord Marcus, but all thoughts of him were erased the second she stepped inside the grandest room she'd ever seen. The walls were paneled mahogany and hung with massive oil paintings of beautiful, aristocratic women in incredible confections of lace and silk, smiling peacefully. There were marble pedestals topped with pure white sculptures of male torsos and heads, and high above, set into the wall that kept out the noise of Park Avenue, was a massive stained-glass window.

"Oh my God!" cried the familiar, shrill voice of Bailey Winter. The dignified Park Avenue designer skipped into the room like a schoolgirl, his yellow-white hair sticking straight up on end as if he'd been electrocuted while using his hair dryer. He was astonishingly short, like a man in miniature, and dressed in a blue blazer with brass buttons, an open shirt, white linen pants, and bare feet stuffed into supple cream-colored leather loafers that made a funny squeaking sound on the hardwood floors. Tied jauntily around his neck was a bold yellow ascot in the same print he'd used in his last collection. "Eleanor Rose, you bitch, you're so skinny!"

"Bailey!" cried Eleanor. They embraced, dropping loud, wet kisses on one another's cheeks.

Mwa, mwa, mwa, mwa!

"And who are these two gorgeous creatures?" Bailey asked, dramatically ripping his signature aviator sunglasses off of his face and cupping his chin in his hand. He inspected Blair and Jasmine intensely. "Fabulous. They're just fabulous, aren't they?" he asked of no one in particular.

"Bailey," Eleanor told him, proudly, "this is my daughter, Blair, and my son Tyler's girlfriend, Jasmine."

"Eek!" Bailey Winter squealed.

Blair had never heard a grown man make a noise like that in her entire life.

"They're incredible," he gushed. "Come on, sit down. Let's get some tea in us and talk things over, shall we, ladies?" The designer beckoned to the butler, waving his palm in the air like it had come loose at the wrist. He led them over to an enormous sectional sofa and froze suddenly. "Psst," he hissed, turning and grinning maniacally at Blair. "*Tea* is just a code word for *martinis*." He winked.

Blair winked back at him, a slow smile spreading across her face. This was not what she'd been expecting.

It was way, *way* better.

will v ever eat lunch in this town again?

"Okay, let's do a take," Ken Mogul said to his first assistant director. He slouched glumly in a tall canvas chair emblazoned with his initials, clenching a chewed-up ballpoint pen in his teeth.

Vanessa focused her camera on the table where she'd be shooting. Fred's, the Barneys restaurant that was central to the action of the movie, was a mob scene. Instead of the usual lunch crowd, the restaurant was flooded with harsh, industrial lighting and crammed full of the hundred-strong *Breakfast at Fred's* crew. They'd moved out most of the chairs and tables to help accommodate everyone, but between the makeup people, prop people, hair people, lighting people, gofers, assistant directors, assistants to the assistant directors, and interns, it was kind of a tight fit.

Just like the shoe department during the end-of-season sale.

"Okay, let's do a take!" the assistant yelled. Everyone scurried away and Ken Mogul waved at Vanessa, who was stationed to his right, peering through the viewfinder of her camera. "Go ahead and roll, Vanessa."

"We're rolling!" Vanessa shouted proudly. She'd always dreamed of saying that, although she'd imagined saying it inside a morgue or some other grim place where her first independent feature would be set. Certainly not in Barneys with

Thaddeus Smith playing the lead. Still, she'd come a long way since directing an adaptation of *War and Peace* for school.

Today was the second day of shooting and they were scheduled to wrap a pivotal dinner scene between Thaddeus, playing Jeremy, and indie starlet Miranda Grace, who was playing Helena, the villain. *Breakfast at Fred's* was the first film she'd made without her twin sister, Coco. Officially, Miranda was striking out on her own, but really, Coco was in rehab. She'd been replaced by a girl named Courtney Pinard Ken had discovered skateboarding in Washington Square Park, who could actually *do* the skating stunts Coco had been too wasted to learn.

On set, Miranda picked up her ice-filled cocktail tumbler, gave it a swirl, then drained it in one sip. She cleared her throat noisily and reached across the table to grab Thaddeus's hand. "Darling, do you believe in fate?" she asked.

Her words echoed around the set, which was quiet enough that Vanessa could make out the tinkling of ice in Miranda's glass.

"I'm not sure what I believe in anymore," Thaddeus responded quietly. "I do know one thing, though." He paused.

This was the moment that Vanessa—that everyone on set—had been dreading. Serena was supposed to burst into the restaurant, trailing a tattered mink stole, and join the couple at their table.

A moment passed. Then another.

No Serena. No Holly. No one.

"Fucking cut!" barked Ken Mogul.

"Cut, everyone," echoed the first assistant director calmly, and suddenly the set came alive: a swarm of makeup people and hair stylists emerged from the shadows, teasing Thaddeus's hair, reapplying gloss to Miranda's lips. A prop assistant refilled the glass Miranda had been swirling, wiping her lipstick from the rim.

"Will someone," Ken whispered, "please tell Miss Fucking van der Fucking Whatever-the-fuck-her-name-is to get on her damn mark and make this fucking picture, please?"

"Sorry, sorry!" called Serena, stumbling onto the set, brandishing a menacing Bailey Winter stiletto. "I was still in wardrobe. I'm sorry, these shoes, they're just—"

"Serena on the set!" cried the second assistant director.

Thanks for the update.

"Holly, Holly, Holly." Ken Mogul shook his head. "To your mark, okay? Let's do this again."

The army of assistants retreated to the shadows and they ran the scene once more. This time, as Thaddeus was on the verge of responding to Miranda's question, Serena burst into the restaurant, right on cue, adjusting the stole that had slipped from her bare shoulder.

"I'm here, I'm here," she chirped, striding past the other tables, swishing her tiered chiffon Bailey Winter dress. She dragged over a chair from an unoccupied table and sat.

"Can I help you?" snapped Miranda.

"Cut, please, cut, right now," Ken Mogul muttered.

"Cut!" cried his loyal loudmouthed assistant.

"Miranda and Serena, please, you're Helena and Holly now. Make us believe it," he said. "Miranda, make me believe that you're a woman who could run the world."

Miranda nodded blankly, batting her fake eyelashes. She was from the Lower East Side. She'd gone to a slutty Catholic school. Her favorite food was Kraft mac & cheese. She clearly had no idea what he was talking about.

Did anyone?

During the third take, everything seemed to come together. Thaddeus and Miranda sparkled, nailing their lines perfectly, even throwing in some ad-libbed business about that day's specials. The lighting looked beautiful and natural, with no accidental glares or twinkles, the sound quality was perfect. And Serena arrived on time, didn't fumble a line or any of her blocking, and when Ken yelled, "Cut!" it was because the scene was in the bag.

"Maybe this won't be so bad after all," the director stage-whispered to Vanessa. "That's it for now, people," he yelled. "Let's take fifteen."

He turned back to Vanessa and said, in a normal tone of voice: "You're up, kid. Let's see what you got."

No problem, Vanessa thought. Things might be all fucked up with everything else—like whatever the hell was going on with Dan—but she knew what to do with a camera.

Ken Mogul dragged his canvas director's chair over to the playback monitor, where he'd be able to screen the footage Vanessa had just shot. Vanessa's assistant camera guy rolled the footage and Vanessa joined the director, watching over his shoulder.

The first time they'd run the scene, Vanessa had used a straightforward angle, moving the camera in and then out to capture the nuances in the performances, but all in all keeping a fairly traditional distance from the actors. It looked wooden and stiff to her; it was clean and tidy but unimaginative. The second time they'd rolled, she'd tried something radically different, zooming in to focus first on Thaddeus's lips and then panning up to examine his eyelashes. She'd used this strategy with his costar, too, to get a rapid-fire, music video effect that was really impressionistic. It was more challenging than what you usually saw in a movie, but it was also better. On the third take she'd gone even further, letting the camera's gaze linger on the ice dancing in the glass of water on the table. She thought it was a fitting way to symbolize the characters' complex relationships with each other. It was some of her best work.

"What the fuck is this?" asked Ken Mogul calmly.

Vanessa looked at him. She couldn't quite read the tone of his voice.

"I asked you a question," Ken repeated, spinning around to face her. "What the fuck was that, Vanessa? What the fuck was *that*?"

"That was my camera work," Vanessa replied, proudly, but her voice was shaking a bit.

"Are you fucking kidding me?" Ken Mogul screamed. Nearby crew members backed into the shadows, and Vanessa could feel all eyes on her.

"Vanessa, what is this experimental bullshit? This is not what I hired you for."

That was *exactly* what he'd hired her for! Those had been his *exact* words, as a matter of fact. Vanessa just stared at him, stunned.

"That's it. This is the last thing I need. I've got an actress who can't act, I'm chewing on fucking ballpoint pens because I'm not allowed to smoke on my own fucking set, and now this: little Miss Indie Film is giving me her bullshit camera work. I don't need this. You're fired!" Ken turned away from Vanessa and settled back into his chair. "And you," he added, pointing to a gofer, "tell Thad, Serena, and Miranda to stay ready. Thanks to this bullshit, we're going to have to reshoot."

Vanessa opened her mouth to respond, but nothing came out. She was angry, freaking fucking angry, but more than that, she was *hurt*. Tears welled in her eyes and her throat felt tight like she had to cough. She couldn't believe what had happened. They'd only just started filming, and she was already fired? First Ruby kicked her out, then Dan went and started acting like some sort of Buddhist asshole, and now *this*?

"Vanessa, what's the matter?" Ken demanded roughly. "You deaf? I said you're fired. Get the hell off my set."

Vanessa stuffed her equipment into her bag and stormed toward the escalator. The first movie she made at NYU was going to be about a freak-show movie director who got maimed by a pack of rabid coyotes. And then got hit by a subway.

See how he likes *that* camera work.

reunited . . . and it feels so good

It was eerie, stepping out of the elevator at Barneys and onto the quiet, dark ninth floor. It was like one of those super-lifelike moments in a really vivid bad dream, when you end up somewhere familiar, but it's all horribly wrong. But this was no nightmare: it was the opposite, really—a dream come true.

Just twenty minutes before, Blair had been innocently taking "tea" with Bailey Winter and her mother, but she'd been dispatched to Barneys before she could drain her first martini.

"Fashion doesn't wait!" Bailey screamed in his girlish tenor. "Go. Go!"

Guess she got the job.

He wanted Blair to dash to Barneys and consult with the *Breakfast at Fred's* on-set costumer, to get the final measurements for the principal cast. The seamstresses in his atelier needed them in order to get the costumes for the climactic party scene ready in time. So far this job had all the makings of a Blair Waldorf fantasy: fashion, glamour, a bit of drama. The only downside was Jasmine.

Oh, right. *Her.*

Bailey Winter had mistaken Tyler's girlfriend for Blair's *friend* and insisted on hiring them *both* to be his eyes and ears on the set. But Blair was not going to let the presence of her young imitator ruin her victory. In fact, she was going to use it to her advantage. Clearly, she could get Jasmine to do her bidding.

She started in the taxi, instructing Jasmine on how to behave when they got to the set. "Let me do the talking. The talent won't like it if you pipe in," Blair directed like an old pro. She'd traded her easily acquired English accent for Hollywood lingo without missing a beat.

Jasmine followed behind Blair like an adoring puppy, out of the elevator and down the black marble ninth-floor hallway toward Fred's. They were marching with such purpose they couldn't help but collide with the black-clad, tear-smeared bald figure who appeared out of nowhere, running at full clip. Vanessa knocked into Blair, who knocked into Jasmine, who was so close on Blair's heels she fell to the ground with a little yelp, her BCBG sandals skittering across the marble floor without her.

"Damn it!" Blair swore before recognizing her old roommate.

"Jesus. Fuck. I'm sorry," Vanessa managed. Her cheeks, even her scalp, were blotchy and there were tears dripping off her chin.

"Are you okay? You're all . . . red," Blair observed lamely. Vanessa was clearly upset, but Blair was supposed to be inside measuring Thaddeus Smith's inseam!

And we all know where the inseam leads. . . .

"I'm okay, I'm okay," muttered Jasmine as she pulled herself back up to her feet, even though no one had been talking to her.

"Jasmine, Vanessa." Blair introduced the two. Then she wrapped her arms around Vanessa and air-kissed her on each cheek. "But really, what's wrong?"

Vanessa just sniffled in response. She was so upset she didn't trust her voice. What was she supposed to do now? Where was she supposed to go?

"Okay, Jasmine," Blair barked, relishing her role as boss. "Stay here and make sure Vanessa's okay. I've got to get moving. Bailey's orders!" She squeezed Vanessa's shoulder in a show of support and smiled weakly. "You know I love you!" she cried, then dashed down the hall and through the swinging doors of Fred's.

"Excuse me," Blair said loudly to no one in particular as soon as she stepped inside. "My name is Blair Waldorf. I work with Bailey Winter. I need to speak to someone in charge here."

No one moved, and no one responded. Then Blair felt a tap on her shoulder and heard a familiar voice.

"I think I can help you," offered Serena.

"Hey." Blair turned to see the grinning face of her best friend. Or were they not friends now? They'd had so many ups and downs it was honestly sometimes hard for Blair to remember if she liked Serena again or if they weren't speaking to each other.

"You're back!" Serena squealed. She grabbed Blair and hugged her tightly.

Looks like friends forever.

"I'm back," Blair echoed, enviously assessing Serena's ebony chiffon Bailey Winter dress.

"Tell me everything," Serena insisted, pulling away from Blair and inspecting her closely. "Since when are you working for Bailey Winter? I thought you were in London!"

"I got a job," Blair explained matter-of-factly. "It just seemed like the responsible thing to do, you know. I thought it would be good to have some career experience under my belt."

"That's great!" Serena practically screamed.

"I've been thinking about a career in fashion," she added casually. The hundred-odd-person crew of *Breakfast at Fred's* gaped at her, just waiting for Ken Mogul to verbally chop off her head. Blair went on in an oblivious loud voice, eating up the attention. "Everyone has a calling, and I think fashion is mine."

"What about London? What about Lord Whatsisname?"

Serena demanded. Were the rumors about his English fiancée actually true? She didn't usually listen to gossip, but there had to be a reason for Blair to give up a royal romance in London to come home and take a summer job.

"It's a long story." Blair sighed dramatically. She was a working woman with a past. Now if Serena would just loan her that dress . . .

"Tell it to me tonight," Serena whispered excitedly. "Ken's putting me up in my own apartment. You should totally come over. Shit, screw that—move in with me!"

"Well . . ." Blair hesitated. She'd moved around a lot lately: the Plaza Hotel, Williamsburg, the Yale Club, London. And wasn't she supposed to be home, close to her baby sister?

"Did I mention that I'm now living on East Seventy-first Street?" Serena knew full well that Blair Waldorf of all people would recognize that address.

Move into the apartment from *Breakfast at Tiffany's*!

"I just need to pack my bags," Blair responded stoically, as if she could hide the fact that she was practically peeing in her pants with excitement. "I'll be there tonight."

She threw her arms around Serena in a fit of impetuous enthusiasm. Everything always had a way of turning out just right, especially when Serena was involved. This time they really would stay friends forever.

If you can call the next few days forever!

karma chameleon

Dan Humphrey slipped into the disgusting employees-only restroom in a dank corner of the basement of the Strand clutching a tiny black tote bag emblazoned with the logo of the literary magazine *Red Herring*. Double-checking that the door was locked tight, he pulled his threadbare Bauhaus T-shirt over his head and unbuttoned his fine-wale Levi's cords, dropping them to the floor. He paid no attention to the literary graffiti a generation of disaffected Strand employees had scrawled all over the walls—legend had it that some bitter former clerk had jotted down the actual New Hampshire home telephone number of the famously reclusive J. D. Salinger. He had only ten minutes to meet Bree in Union Square and he had to get out of his everyday clothes—which reeked of smoke—and into something cleaner and more exercise-friendly.

So he wasn't the most athletic guy in the world. His relationship or connection or whatever with Bree was based on more than Lycra clothing and naked yoga sessions. Bree had opened Dan's eyes, helped him think about the world in a way he never had before. Bending and posing in a hot room with a sweaty naked guy leaning into him wasn't Dan's idea of a romantic evening, but reading Bree's favorite books was stimulating and thought-provoking. He'd done so much in his life already—had a poem published in the *New Yorker*, interned at *Red Herring*, sung his original songs with the Raves—but it was kind of thrilling to discover something deeper and more meaningful than fleeting fame.

Finding enlightenment in less than a week—it must be some kind of world record.

He pulled a clean, bright green American Apparel T-shirt over his head, smoothed out his tousled light brown hair, and laced up his ice-blue New Balances. He popped a piece of icy mint gum into his mouth and exhaled into the palm of his hand to double-check his breath: not a trace of tobacco. He wadded up his work clothes and stashed them in his employee locker, then jogged up the stairs and out of the store, toward nearby Union Square.

Bree was waiting for him near the statue of a placidly smiling Gandhi in the southwest corner of the bustling park near skanky-but-getting-better Fourteenth Street. "I like to go there sometimes," she'd told him over the phone. "To read and reflect on Gandhi's message of peace."

Don't we all?

Bree had braided her platinum blond hair and wound it tightly into a bun at the base of her neck. She was sporting a clean white T-shirt emblazoned with the Adidas logo and iridescent blue running shorts that were cropped short and showcased her well-muscled, lean, long legs. When she spied Dan, she stood and waved excitedly.

"Right on time!" When he reached her, she threw her arms around him in a warm embrace. "Namaste," she whispered. "You smell nice."

"Thanks," Dan responded with relief as he inadvertently breathed in the bouquet of Bree's organic sage deodorant and the patchouli oil she wore dabbed behind each ear.

"Let's get warmed up," Bree ordered. She released Dan from her embrace, turned, and put her right foot on the bench where she'd just been sitting, then leaned in, shifting all her weight to that leg.

Dan imitated her, wincing in pain as he tried to awaken the

muscles in his legs. This was a lot more demanding than his usual workout: a walk to the corner for smokes.

"Feels great, huh?" Bree grinned enthusiastically while she stretched, as though a good stretch was better than a hot bath.

"Yeah," Dan wheezed. "Excellent."

"I thought we'd start here," Bree explained, putting her feet back on the ground. She locked her knees, then reached down, touching the ground with both palms. "You know, head across Fourteenth Street to the Hudson and then downtown to Battery Park."

Dan did some mental math. That was at least two miles, which was two miles farther than he'd ever jogged in his life.

What had he gotten himself into?

At first it seemed like he was going to be fine: the first block went by without incident. Dan followed the sexy wiggle of Bree's ass as she jogged down the sidewalk, dodging pedestrians and strollers.

This is fun! he told himself. *It feels great.*

When they reached the corner of Fifth Avenue, they paused for the light, and Bree turned to him. "Are you okay?" She furrowed her brow in worry.

Dan's skin felt prickly. The sweat poured off of his forehead and down his nose, dripping on the sidewalk. The early evening sun was beating down on them. He was pretty sure he'd be dead by sundown.

"Sure," he responded shakily. "I'm fine."

When they'd been moving, the burn in his legs and the pounding in his chest had been somehow bearable, but as soon as they'd stopped his knees had felt like they might buckle underneath him.

The light changed and Bree dashed into the street. "Come on!" she called over her shoulder happily.

Dan took a deep breath and stumbled into the street, just missing running over an old lady in a big straw hat, pulling a shopping trolley.

"Watch it, asshole!" she shouted.

Ignoring her, Dan kept running, following Bree like a dog at the track chasing that mechanical rabbit. His heart pounded in his ears as they jogged down the sidewalk past Sixth, then Seventh, Eighth, and, finally, Ninth Avenues. Between Ninth and Greenwich the traffic cleared, so Bree ran in the street. Ignoring the hot blasts of exhaust from the oncoming buses, Dan followed behind, jogging toward the shimmering Hudson River, just two blocks away.

Hang in there, he told himself. *Just make it to the river. Just keep going.* He had no idea how he'd make it all the way down to Battery Park, on the tip of Manhattan, but first things first: he had to get to the river. His feet throbbed inside his not-quite-broken-in ice blue New Balance bought-for-ten-bucks-at-the-Paragon-Sports-sale running shoes. He'd wiped so much sweat from his forehead that he was scared that he might be completely dehydrated. He was dying for a drink of water. He was dying to sit down.

Maybe he was just plain *dying*?

They dashed across the West Side Highway and into Hudson River Park, where a wide, paved jogging/rollerblading/bike path ran from midtown to Tribeca. They weren't the only ones taking advantage of the clear, sunny day—hundreds of people were running and rollerblading, bicycling, and strolling hand in hand. Bree beat him across the street and wove through the crowd until she reached the chain-link fence that presumably kept people from diving right into the river. She kicked her legs up in front of her, jogging in place as she waited for Dan to catch up. Despite the heat, she was barely sweating.

Dan hurled himself in Bree's direction. *This is great*, he told himself. He felt great! The sun was bright, the air was fresh, and there was a breeze blowing in off the river. He grinned wildly. He could do this!

Then his legs gave way underneath him and he landed on

the rough pavement with a thud as he crumpled to the ground.

"Dan!" Bree cried, leaning over him. "Are you okay?"

Dan looked up to see her flushed face framed by wispy ringlets of flaxen hair. His vision started to cloud.

"Am I dying?" he asked out loud. "Are you an angel?"

"I better administer CPR," Bree announced sternly, crouching down and pressing her mouth to his.

As if that wouldn't give him an even bigger heart attack.

from the frying pan to the fire

Wobbling uneasily, Vanessa Abrams gripped the wrought-iron railing and steadied herself on the low marble steps leading up to the ivy-covered mansion on Eighty-seventh Street. She burped noisily and jabbed at the illuminated doorbell four or five times before she finally managed to ring it. Maybe consoling herself with an ice-cold bottle of pinot grigio hadn't been the wisest decision she'd ever made, especially since she was minutes away from a job interview.

After being unceremoniously thrown off the set of *Breakfast at Fred's*, Vanessa had ridden the elevator with the possibly humanoid Blair-Waldorf-in-training Jasmine, who had informed Vanessa that it just so happened that her mother was looking for a highly qualified, energetic, and enthusiastic person for a very important job. Vanessa had been too upset to get the exact details, but Jasmine tore a page from her Louis Vuitton agenda and scribbled an address, urging Vanessa to follow up on it immediately.

After a few glasses of wine pilfered from Rufus Humphrey's personal stash, Vanessa had started to see things more clearly.

Ken Mogul is a soulless sellout. He was making a run-of-the-mill Hollywood teen soap while she was an experimental auteur! She had no business wasting her time and her talent on that crap. She was bound for NYU, the best film program in the country. She'd have access to the finest professors, world-class equipment, and an entire acting program full of the most talented student actors around. Why should she be wasting her time as a hack, working on a project she didn't believe in when she could be working her ass off and saving up the cold hard cash to produce her own film in the fall. She already had an idea for a feature, about a conflicted young artist forced to choose between following her muse or staying in a rapidly decaying relationship with her insane incense-and-herbal-tea-addicted writer boyfriend.

Sounds like a case of art imitating life.

A sour-faced maid in an honest-to-God black skirt with white apron and little white lace doily on her head opened the heavy glass door. "Can I help you?" she demanded suspiciously.

"I'm here about the job," Vanessa slurred. "The mom's daughter," she paused momentarily fumbling with the girl's name. "Jasmine! That's it. She told me to come and see her mom about a job. So I did."

The maid frowned. "I see. Come in then. The lady of the house will meet you in her office."

Vanessa stomped through the marble foyer, past a sweeping staircase illuminated by a massive crystal chandelier, and into a mahogany-paneled room lined with bookcases and furnished with tasteful antiques. She had no idea what the job in question was, but clearly this was a very successful businesswoman. She was probably a busy executive in desperate need of a competent personal assistant. It was sure to be shit work, but artists always had to suffer for their art, unless they wanted to make commercial shit like Ken Mogul.

"Please wait here," the maid instructed.

Vanessa perched on the edge of an ornate Art Deco wood chair. The room was ever-so-slightly spinning, and she gripped the seat tightly. *Just don't throw up*, she told herself.

"You my new friend?"

Vanessa looked up. There was no one there.

Great, I'm so trashed I'm hearing voices.

"You my new friend?" asked the voice again before dissolving into giggles.

"Wh-who's there?" Vanessa called out nervously. The last thing she wanted was to be caught talking to herself in front of her new boss.

"Are you a girl?" another voice asked.

"Why don't you have any hair?" asked the first voice.

Two voices? How much had she had to drink?

Vanessa held her breath and listened. She stood up. Where were the voices coming from? She knelt and pressed her cheek to the cold, perfectly polished wood floor, scanning the room from that vantage. It worked: under the gilded wood couch she could make out the figure of a skinny little boy with taut curly hair.

"You found me!" he cried, clambering out from under the couch.

"Yeah, hi," Vanessa said. "Is your mommy home?"

"You smell like wine," the boy announced, frowning. "I'm four. How old are you?"

"Find me too!" cried the other voice.

What could she do?

"Where are you?" she called out, propping herself up on her hands and knees. She looked under the other furniture.

"Find me, find me!" the voice called.

She followed the sound of the voice to the corner of the library, where a large globe stood on a round glass-topped table. She lifted the tablecloth, and underneath was a little boy who looked, and was dressed, exactly like the other kid.

"You found me!" the boy cried. He dashed out from under the table and ran over to the couch, where his brother was still bouncing. He leaped onto the couch and rammed into his brother. The two boys tumbled onto the floor.

"Boys!" called a voice. A tall, magenta-pink-Chanel-suit-clad redheaded woman strode into the library, clutching a Treo and a rolled up copy of *Vogue*.

"You must be Vanessa," the woman observed in a clipped tone. "Jasmine mentioned you might be calling. I'm a little surprised you've decided to just drop by, but I suppose that's fine. Shows initiative. I like that."

Oops.

"Right," Vanessa said, standing up and trying her best to appear completely sober. "You must be Mrs. . . . ?" She paused, realizing that she had no idea what Jasmine's last name was.

"It's Ms. Morgan," the woman replied. "I didn't take my husband's name. This is the twenty-first century, after all."

"Sorry," Vanessa mumbled. This was the weirdest job interview ever.

"No matter," the woman continued. "You're clearly a hit with the boys."

"The boys?" Vanessa asked. The twins came up behind her, pulling on her hands with all their might.

"Play with us!" they cried.

"So, you know, the job is fairly standard." Ms. Morgan fiddled with her Treo for a moment. "A few days a week, just in the afternoons. You'll fetch the boys from camp, run them to their therapist, accompany them on their playdates, the usual sort of thing. No doubt you know the drill." She put the phone to her ear.

Camp? *Playdates*? Excuse me?

"I think there's been some misunderstanding," Vanessa stammered, struggling to stay upright with the wine in her system and the weight of two kids tugging her floorward. Suffering for her art was all well and good, but she was no Mrs. Doubtfire.

"Yay!" the twins cried. "Mommy, is Vanessa our new friend?"

"Yes," the woman answered, her ear still glued to the over-size phone. "She's your new friend."

She was?

"It's eighteen dollars an hour," Ms. Morgan added as she clicked out into the foyer and up the grand staircase. "You can start right now."

Oh yeah, she definitely *is*.

b and s decide it's share and share alike

She'd made three trips back and forth, but Blair still hadn't managed to get all of her bags up the five flights of stairs. There wasn't a doorman, there wasn't any air conditioning, there wasn't an elevator, but she didn't mind because the whole thing was just so . . . cinematic.

Blair had a plan for her life, a script she wanted to follow exactly. But so much of what had happened so far—buying a wedding gown, leaving Lord Marcus, getting hired by Bailey Winter, and now moving in with Serena—wasn't planned. If someone had told her just a week before that she'd have to get a job for the summer, she'd have screamed and protested—working for the summer was definitely not part of the story of her life—but Blair didn't feel like screaming. She felt . . . happy. Maybe there was a lesson here; maybe instead of trying to always live according to a plan, she should just go with the flow? Maybe things really did always work out in the end.

Just like in the movies.

Bounding down the last flight of steps to retrieve her very last bag—a crocodile Paul Smith duffel she'd picked up in London only a couple of days before—Blair was startled by the lanky, dark-haired guy wearing a crisp blue Hugo Boss suit, stepping out of the parlor-floor apartment. She froze in her tracks.

Isn't there a handsome downstairs neighbor in *Breakfast at Tiffany's*?

"Hello there," Blair called out in her best vaguely Eastern European, Audrey-Hepburn-as-Holly-Golightly accent.

"Hey," the guy responded shyly. His tousled brown hair hung down in front of his blue eyes. He tucked his hands in the pockets of his suit pants and pulled himself up to full height.

"Good evening," Blair replied, strolling down the stairs primly through the narrow, badly lit space that passed for a lobby. She squeezed past the smiling stranger and bent to pick up her bag. "Excuse me," she continued, heaving the bag full of shoes onto her shoulder.

"Of course," he said, leaning his back against the door to his apartment. "Can I help you with that?"

"I can manage it," Blair told him stoically. She flashed her most charming smile. "Have we met?"

"I'm Jason." He extended his hand. "You visiting for the weekend?"

"Oh," she explained, "I'm moving in with my dear old friend Serena. On the fifth floor?"

"Oh, I know Serena." Jason paused. "We hung out the other night, drank some beers on the stoop. She never mentioned anything about her beautiful roommate, though."

And she'd never mentioned her handsome new neighbor either.

Typical.

"It was a bit spur of the moment," Blair explained. "It's a long story."

"I've got time." His lips spread into a cute, flirtatious little grin. He tucked his long fingers into his back pockets. "And I'm a great listener."

"Is that so?" Blair shifted the bag from one shoulder to the other. It *was* sort of heavy.

"Not only that," Jason continued, "I was just on my way out to pick up a nice cold bottle of rosé. Have you been up to the roof yet? Maybe you'd like to join me for a welcome-to-the-building drink?"

"I didn't know we could get up there!" A cool glass of pink wine with a broad-shouldered, blue-eyed stranger sounded like the perfect way to celebrate the end of a milestone of a day: new job, new house . . .

New romance?

Serena was busy memorizing her lines for tomorrow. A drink with Jason would keep Blair out of her hair.

"I know a way," he said, winking. "I'll meet you in fifteen minutes?"

Under normal circumstances that would hardly have been enough time for Blair Waldorf to prepare herself for an evening tête-à-tête, but this was the new and improved, girl-with-a-job, ever-fashion-ready, easygoing summertime Blair Waldorf.

"I'll give you ten." She skipped up the stairs slowly turning back to smile at him. "By the way, I'm Blair."

After throwing on a casual pink floral Lilly Pulitzer tunic top and some white shell-embellished flip-flops, Blair headed upstairs. Jason was already waiting for her with a blanket slung over his shoulder and a bottle clutched in his hand. He scaled the rusty ladder and pushed open the black steel trapdoor. Then he reached down to help Blair up with more studly grace than Marcus had ever shown. Blair grabbed his hand eagerly and let him pull her up to the rooftop.

"I hope it doesn't rain tonight," she remarked as she twirled around, taking in three hundred and sixty degrees of Manhattan skyline view. "Because I'm never going *down* that ladder." She was only half-kidding.

"I told you the view was great," Jason teased, digging a wine key into the cork and pulling it out with a satisfying pop.

It wasn't as commanding as the view of Central Park from the high-up terrace of Blair's Fifth Avenue penthouse, but there was something magical about the hot summer haze lingering over the neighborhood's bland apartment towers. The trees weren't as perfectly pruned as the oaks and elms that surrounded the park, but the spindly branches that peeked above the roofline were lush and green. The Upper East Side, Blair realized, was just like Bailey Winter's line: from Fifth to Park Avenues was Bailey Winter Couture, everything from the Park to Lexington was like Bailey Winter Collection, and everything between there and the river was Bailey by Bailey Winter.

That's one way to think of it.

"It's really nice," she agreed, taking a plastic cup of chilled wine and settling onto the worn navy blue cotton blanket Jason had spread on the warm tar roof. It wasn't as soft as her favorite cashmere Asprey picnic throw, but she had on the perfect summer outfit, a gorgeous man was sitting next to her, and her career in fashion was about to explode. Who needed minor British royalty? She was a New Yorker and this was a classic summer-in-New-York moment. London was a damp and smelly slum by comparison.

"So, how come Serena never mentioned you before?" Jason asked.

"Maybe she wanted you all to herself," Blair replied mischievously and probably accurately. "To a crazy summer." Blair clinked her plastic cup of wine with Jason's. "So far," she added giddily.

"To a crazy summer," he echoed, taking a sip. "Anyway, I don't think Serena's interested in me. We hung out the other night and she seemed sort of spoken for, if you know what I mean."

"You mean Thaddeus Smith?" Blair and Serena hadn't had much time to catch up but she knew, just *knew*, that there had to be something going on between Serena and Thaddeus.

Since she and everyone else believe everything they read.

"The one and only," Jason affirmed. "But you know, Blair," Jason continued, fixing his blue eyes on hers. "I'm not really into hanging out with movie stars. I like regular girls."

Was he calling her—Blair Waldorf—*regular*? How wrong he was.

"Wait, you're not in the movies, are you?" He eyed her suspiciously. "Because you look like you could be."

"I'm more of a behind-the-scenes kind of girl," she murmured, batting her Chanel-mascara-blackened eyelashes mysteriously.

"I don't have anything against it," Jason backtracked. "Don't get me wrong. It's just that I'm interested in different things. Like the law. That's my main focus, you know?"

"I was thinking of studying law when I start at Yale in the fall." She could always be a lawyer *and* a fashion muse at the same time. She could wear couture under her Supreme Court gown.

"Beautiful and smart," Jason said. "You're almost too good to be true."

Blair sipped her wine hungrily. Serena could have the movie star. Jason was exactly the kind of guy a Yale woman *should* be involved with.

At least, the kind of woman a Yale woman should be involved with this week.

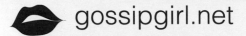

Disclaimer: All the real names of places, people, and events have been altered or abbreviated to protect the innocent. Namely, me.

hey people!

I'm not ashamed to admit that "Summer Lovin'" (from our secret favorite I'm-staying-in-Friday-night movie, *Grease*) is one of the best songs I've ever heard. Not only is it catchy, it's true: summer is all about love and gettin' some lovin', right? But there seems to be a shortage this summer.

It's been almost three weeks and our friend **S** is still a solo performer! What gives? Sure, she's been spotted around town with **T**, but there's no law that friends can't have dinner together, now is there? Besides, we think **T** might have his eye on someone else. You heard it here first.

Meanwhile, **B** is throwing herself into her work—word is she's already the second–most feared person on that movie set. We haven't gotten close enough to verify the rumors that she's sporting an engagement ring on her right hand—to throw off the paparazzi, just like the stars. Word also has it that **B's** looking a little rosy in the cheeks: mother-to-be flush, secret love, or great new facialist? Break out your camera phones, people: we need evidence!

More summer-lovin' updates: it seems **D** and **V** are definitely on the outs, and again, you heard it here first. He's looking surprisingly tan and toned. Owearoiool And what about **N** and his summer lover? How long till he shows his true city-boy colors? He might say he's not like the rest of the city crowd, but **N** can only forsake creature comforts like nightclub bottle service, black-tie fundraisers on Lilypond Lane, and private helicopter rides back to the city for so long. . . .

trouble brewing

My spies at Michael's have tipped me off about a very tense meeting between a certain highly respected photographer-turned-filmmaker and the Hollywood heavyweights (literally a pair of rotund brothers) who are bankrolling his latest venture. It seems that the deep-pocketed producers are less than thrilled with the dailies and want to rethink the casting. Could this mean that **V** won't be the only one to get canned? Stay tuned.

sightings

B, Frappuccino and clipboard in hand, desperately trying to hail a cab on Park Avenue. Whatever happened to that graduation present? Is it true that she doesn't actually have her license? Oops! **N** at the Amagansett farmer's market, deliberating over the wildflowers. We knew he was a closet romantic! **T** showing an unidentified special guest around the set—we hear the private tour included a lengthy visit to the star's trailer. **V** at Forbidden Planet, stocking up on comic books—but definitely not visiting **D** at the Strand, which is, after all, just right across the street. Interesting . . .

and they call it puppy love . . .

Speaking of love, I've finally met someone. Actually, two someones: they're both irresistibly adorable and neither can stop showering me with kisses. I know it's wrong to come between brothers, but I could never choose between my dear Luke and Owen.

You might have seen that big story about them in last week's Sunday Styles: they're puggles, the only hybrid for me: half beagle, half pug, but 100 percent love. And mine just happen to have come from the shelter. I'm a sucker for strays with impeccable breeding. It's the new couture for a cause, so

don't waste your time with some haughty Chihuahua or a
slobbery French bulldog.

your e-mail

Dear GG,
I'm a paralegal at a law firm in Midtown and I've been
dying over one of my coworkers for weeks. He used to
come out with us for happy hour, but suddenly he's
turned totally homebody—he practically runs back to
his apartment after work. Do you think it's something
embarrassing, like a porn addiction?
—Crushed

Dear Crushed,
Sounds like he's definitely addicted to something—or
someone—at home. But there's only one good reason a
happy-hour hottie turns stay-at-home stud: a girl. Here's
my advice: offer to tie him up with his new mallard-print tie
and see what he says. Yes = porn addiction. No, thanks =
girlfriend. Good luck!
—GG

What else is happening out there, people? Send me the scoop:
hot gossip, the latest sample sales, the location of that new
secret As Four boutique, the dirt on the set. And can someone
please tell me the date and location of the totally top-secret
Breakfast at Fred's wrap party? I'll need to reserve a preparty
coiffing with Mr. Fekkai himself, of course. So spill!

You know you love me.

gossip girl

n hits the town

"Fuck you all very much!" The British-born lead singer of the jokingly named Sunshine Experience wiped a hand across his brow and flung his sweat into the crowd. Bare-chested and clad only in tight black leather pants, the scrawny singer, who was better known for squiring models and actresses than actually singing, spat angrily onto the stage and stormed off, disappearing into the thick crowd of revelers.

"God, I love them!" Tawny cried, squeezing Nate's upper thigh and inadvertently spilling half of her Smirnoff sea breeze on the Ultrasuede banquette and her faux-Pucci print XOXO capri pants.

What a pity.

Nate nodded and took a swig of his third pint of Newcastle brown ale of the night. He glanced around the packed main room of Resort, the East Hampton nightclub: the dance floor was teeming with blond girls in Diane von Furstenberg dresses and perfectly groomed stockbroker types in khakis and Thomas Pink shirts—not exactly the type of crowd you'd normally see at a Sunshine Experience show.

The Hamptons had been abuzz with word of this "surprise" show by the English punk band for a week now, and when Tawny suggested they go, Nate's enthusiasm surprised even him. He hadn't made it out to Resort yet that summer—in fact, he hadn't really done much of anything besides clean out gutters, cut grass, fix shingles, and smoke weed with Tawny. It felt good to get out, to be where the action was, with a cold beer and a hot blonde and nothing to worry about.

"Archibald!"

Tawny nudged Nate gently with her elbow. "Is that a friend of yours?"

Anthony Avuldsen wove through the crowd, lifting his whiskey and soda high into the air to avoid a spill. He'd shaved his blond hair close to his head and had a deep summertime tan that made his smile seem even brighter than usual. The bouncer—a burly guy with no discernible neck—gave him a quick nod, allowing him to step up onto the platform that doubled as the club's VIP room.

"Archibald, you son of a bitch," Anthony said, knocking his glass against Nate's bottle in greeting. "Where the hell have you been keeping yourself?"

"Hey," Nate greeted him.

"Coach working you?" Anthony plopped next to Nate on the banquette, nodding his head in time to the thumping bass line.

"Something like that," Nate admitted.

"Dude," Anthony continued, shouting to be heard over the deafening din of the music. "I hear Blair's back in town. What's the story?"

Nate frowned, then draped an arm around Tawny, pulling her even closer. "I don't know." He shrugged.

"I'm Tawny," the girl said, leaning across Nate's lap and smiling in Anthony's direction.

"What's up?" Anthony nodded in greeting. "Anthony."

"You two know each other from school?" she wanted to know.

"Yeah," Anthony responded. "How do you two know each other?"

Nate signaled to the waitress. He needed another drink, immediately.

"Nate just fell at my feet one day," Tawny replied, draining the last of her cocktail. "I guess I'm just lucky."

Anthony studied her, then yelled at Nate, "You're the lucky one, bastard."

The waitress approached, looking exactly like Jessica Simpson playing Daisy in *The Dukes of Hazzard*. "Another round?" she asked.

"Please," Nate told her. If Anthony was going to ask him any more questions, he'd need to get a stronger buzz on.

"I haven't seen you around the city," Anthony continued. "Where do you go to school?"

"Oh, I'm not from the city," Tawny explained. "I live in Hampton Bays."

"Cool," Anthony exclaimed. "I don't think I've ever met a townie before."

Nate jabbed Anthony roughly with his elbow.

"What?" Anthony demanded. "It's cool. No offense, man."

"What?" asked Tawny, cupping her palm over her ear. "It's so loud!"

"Dude," Anthony continued, oblivious. "Isabel is having a party tomorrow. I heard Serena's going to be there. You seen her lately?"

The last time Nate had seen Serena, he'd been kissing Jenny at Blair's graduation party. It was just a "for old times' sake" kiss, but he was pretty sure she and Blair had bonded over how mad at him they were.

What else is new?

Nate shook his head. He felt completely out of touch with all the people he'd grown up with.

"Wait, *Serena*?" asked Tawny excitedly, leaning across Nate's lap. From this vantage he had an unobstructed view down her blouse to her pierced navel and could see *everything* in between. "As in, Serena with the foreign-sounding last name?"

She leaned further forward, giving Nate another glimpse of the Promised Land.

Is she doing that on purpose? Nate wondered.

Nate glanced at Anthony to make sure he wasn't sneaking a peek as well, but he'd turned to talk to some dark-haired beauty Nate vaguely remembered went to Grafton and was a year younger than them.

"I guess so," Nate allowed, enjoying Tawny's surprised expression. Did Serena's name sound foreign? He'd never noticed. But forget Serena—Tawny was clearly impressed. He didn't feel that way often; girls thought he was cute or cool or popular or whatever, but she was looking at him with something he'd never really seen in Blair or Serena's eyes. She looked . . . *awed.*

"We kind of used to see each other," Nate bragged. That was the truth, but it didn't quite cover it.

"Nate Archibald!" Tawny cried, leaning across the table once more, pushing her breasts together invitingly. "You are such a mystery man."

"You know Serena, too?" Anthony leaned back into the conversation, clearly trying to get a sneak peek down Tawny's shirt. "There's going to be some kind of blowout when that movie wraps in a couple days. You should totally come!" he yelled over the booming music.

"You mean *Breakfast at Fred's*?" Tawny looked like her eyes were going to pop out of her head. "I am, like, Thaddeus Smith's number one fan. *Ever!*"

The waitress returned with their drinks and Nate grabbed his greedily.

"I don't know." He shook his head. All of a sudden he felt like he was treading water in a really dark, deep pool. His thinking was a little cloudy from a pre-going-out joint and the three beers, but even in that state he knew it wasn't such a great idea to show up at Serena's wrap party with Tawny on his arm. Blair would definitely be there, and he didn't want her to think that he'd already moved on.

But hadn't he? And hadn't *she?*

"Please," Tawny begged. "I'd *die* to meet Thaddeus Smith. *Die!*"

"Dude," Anthony teased. "Can't say no to a pretty girl."

Nate Archibald never could never say no. Period.

b takes charge

The bang of the slammed door echoed off the walls of the underfurnished apartment. It was hard to stomp in angrily after climbing all those stairs—and in rubber flip-flops, no less—but Serena did her best, stomping on the wood floor, dropping her oversize white leather Jil Sander duffel without a thought for the iPod Nano and glass Dolce & Gabbana sunglasses inside.

"You home, roomie?" Blair called from inside the apartment's one bedroom, which they'd decided to share. They were basically sisters anyway.

They certainly fought like they were.

"Yeah," Serena called back. She grabbed a Corona from the fridge and perched on the windowsill overlooking the back of the town house, her feet dangling out of the window over the fire escape.

"How was work?" Blair strolled into the kitchen wrapped up in a massive white Frette towel she'd swiped from her mom's well-stocked linen closet. She pulled a pack of Merits from Serena's abandoned purse and used the gas stove to light one.

"Work was work." Serena stared glumly down through the slats of the fire escape at the slate backyard below. She sighed. "Honestly, Blair, it kind of sucks."

"What do you mean?" Blair's workday had consisted of

running fabric samples from the tailor on Thirty-ninth Street to Bailey Winter's home, where he was enjoying a "tea" party and private fitting with a Saudi princess.

Blair pushed open the window next to Serena's and leaned outside. She exhaled a plume of smoke into the wind and glanced over at Serena. The breeze blew her blond hair gently as she swung her bare feet and frowned.

"I don't know," Serena sighed, chugging her beer. It had been one of her worst rehearsal days to date. She'd overheard some of the crew members calling her Holly Go Slightly, and then Ken had yelled, "Fuck, fuck, fuck!" right in the middle of her scene. "It's been a long day."

"Tell me everything," Blair urged.

Serena hesitated. They'd never really discussed it, but she knew Blair well enough to know that she wasn't exactly thrilled that Serena was starring in *Breakfast at Fred's*. It was Blair's lifelong dream, after all, not Serena's; how would Blair react to hearing Serena complain about it?

"I'm having some trouble getting this whole acting thing down," Serena admitted sheepishly.

That's an understatement.

"I thought I could do it. I mean, I did it before, but that was different, without lots of experts and people running around on set, watching you, and without that big, huge camera just staring at you like, like . . . like Darth Vader or something."

"Tell me more." Blair leaned out of the window, exhaling smoke into the hot summer night. She loved helping other people with their problems.

More like she just wanted to hear that other people *had* problems.

"I can't do it," complained Serena. She frowned down at her Marc Jacobs flip-flops. "It's just not connecting."

"Serena," Blair murmured dreamily, "you know what you look like?"

"Huh?" Serena looked up. Blair was leaning out the window, still clad only in her towel, clutching a cigarette but not smoking it, so her ash was almost an inch long. She looked like a crazed Madison Avenue maven in an alcoholic trance.

"You look exactly," Blair said, "I mean, *exactly*, like Holly Golightly. The fire escape, the wisps of hair, the light—it's all perfect. It's fucking creepy almost."

"Thanks," Serena uttered. It was one of the nicest things Blair had said to her in their many years of friendship.

"I'm serious," Blair proclaimed. "I'm an expert. I'm in the business, okay? I know about fashion, I know about looks, I know about glamour, and you've got it. I don't care what Ken Mogul might say: you *are* Holly Golightly," she continued determinedly, "if I have anything to do with it."

"What do you mean?" Serena demanded.

"Who is the world's greatest Holly Golightly expert?" Blair asked.

Serena laughed. "You are, no question."

"Well, you're pretty damn lucky to know me, then, aren't you?" Blair remarked. If *she* couldn't be Holly Golightly, well, then she could make Serena into her. That would be satisfaction enough. "Come on." She stubbed out her cigarette and grabbed her friend's hand. "We have work to do."

Their first stop was obvious: the sidewalk outside of Tiffany.

Blair had thrown on a vaguely Mexican embroidered cami she'd bought the previous summer at Scoop and a pair of jeans and had insisted that Serena dress down too. When the cab pulled up in front of the store, Blair practically shoved Serena out into the street.

"Now," Blair barked. "Let me see your walk." Blair stationed herself in front of the store windows and faced her friend. With the traffic zooming past behind her and the tall buildings rising into the sky, Serena looked very small, very vulnerable. Very un-Serena. Very, very un-Holly.

Serena strolled awkwardly toward the store, taking funny little half-steps like a flower girl in a wedding.

"Stop!" Blair howled. She walked out into the middle of the sidewalk. "What was that?"

"What do you mean?" Serena was barely audible over the roar of traffic and the chatter of all the shoppers and tourists milling around.

"You're not trying," Blair intoned, channeling a tough but lovable coach from some inspirational sports movie she'd seen on HBO. "Show me, show me, show me! I *know* you can do a more convincing walk."

"I feel so stupid," Serena admitted. "Everyone's looking at me and I feel all weird and self-conscious."

Miss Dancing-on-the-banquette-at-Bungalow-8, self-conscious?

"You can't feel that way," Blair snapped. "You've got to feel confident. You've got to feel cool. You've got to feel like the whole world is at your disposal, like you're calling the shots, like you're in charge."

And this was called *acting*?

"But I'm just supposed to walk?" Serena asked. This wasn't like walking in a fashion show—which she'd done, of course. "I feel silly."

"Pretend it's graduation again," Blair suggested, remembering Serena's irksome, last-minute dash down the aisle of Brick Church, wearing the exact same Oscar de la Renta suit Blair was wearing.

"I'll try," Serena sighed.

Blair returned to her station in front of Tiffany. She had a lot of work to do, but she had to admit it was kind of fun bossing Serena around for a change.

All in the name of friendship.

just another manic sunday in the park with v . . . and d

With Nils tugging at her left hand and Edgar pulling on her right—or was it Nils on the right and Edgar on the left?—Vanessa Abrams remembered why it was never a good idea to have two boys vying for one girl's attention.

Like she hadn't already learned *that* lesson.

"Come on, come on," complained one of the boys—who cared which one anymore? Their tiny hands were sticky, their little-boy voices whiny, and besides that they were *strong*. They had grips of steel, and since they refused to slow down, Vanessa was half walking and half being dragged along Central Park's shady asphalt paths. It reminded her of the times she and Aaron had walked his fawn-and-white purebred boxer, Mookie, together, except the twins were even more eager to get outside than that dog had been. If they'd had tails, they'd have been wagging them insanely.

"Christ," muttered Vanessa. "Slow down, please!"

Eighteen dollars an hour, eighteen dollars an hour. She'd already made thirty-six dollars that day; not a fortune, but it would go right in the coffers for her next project.

How about her next *apartment*?

Vanessa stumbled a little as the boys stopped short in front of an umbrella-covered cart.

"Can we get ice cream sandwiches?"

She highly doubted that their mother had ever in her life

taken the kids to the park, let alone bought them ice cream. Vanessa hadn't even set eyes on her since their bizarre job interview, and Ms. Morgan didn't seem like the kind of woman who would tolerate ice cream dripping on her bouclé Chanel suits. The Abramses had always kept her and Ruby on a strict sugar-free diet when they were kids, preferring Tofutti and fruit to ice cream and candy, but she didn't care what these two ate.

"Sure, ice cream sandwiches, whatever, you got it," she agreed, wriggling free of the boys' death grips and pulling a crumpled twenty out of her jeans pocket. "Three ice cream sandwiches, please," she told the vendor, who had a handlebar moustache and was wearing a tie-dyed T-shirt circa 1972.

The boys leapt up and down, grabbing at the ice cream. They tore the wrappers open hungrily, then raced away into the confines of the playground, screaming and laughing through gooey mouthfuls of ice cream.

"Wait up!" Vanessa yelled after them halfheartedly. She wasn't sure she cared if they disappeared and she lost her job and went to prison. Had it really been only three days since she'd started work as the principal cinematographer on a major Hollywood production? Or was this whole thing some kind of horrible nightmare?

She sank onto a bench under a tall, gracious oak and watched the twins scarf down their treats and toss their wrappers onto the ground. Oops. Then they started a dizzying game of tag, racing under the slide, between the swings, narrowly avoiding collisions with teetering prewalkers and their menacing minders.

"Stay close!" Vanessa called out weakly. She finished her ice cream and leaned back onto the surprisingly comfortable wood-and-concrete bench. Cars whizzed by on their way through the park at Ninety-seventh Street, a nice, sleep-inducing sound. The sun was strong but there was plenty of shade, and for one brief second she almost didn't mind that she was there as a nanny, not just as some other adult enjoying the park on a nice Sunday afternoon. Her eyes closed and she tuned out for a moment.

Then she heard a familiar high-pitched yelp and her eyes flew open.

Who knew she had a maternal instinct?

There was a commotion not far in the distance, and Vanessa recognized two familiar blond heads.

She got to her feet and hurried over to where one of the twins was sprawled out on the sidewalk, clutching his skinned knee and crying. His brother stood at his side, pointing an angry finger at a rollerblader lying prone on the sidewalk.

"What's going on?" Vanessa demanded, trying to sound authoritative.

"That big boy ran into Edgar!" cried Nils.

A freckle-faced blond nymphet cheerleader type in hot pink short shorts and a complicated electric blue sports bra rolled athletically up to the scene. "What's going on," she snapped, "is that you're not controlling your kids, and we're trying to get some exercise here!"

"They're not *my* kids," Vanessa retorted, kneeling to pat the sobbing Edgar on his head. "And you don't have to be rude."

"Vanessa, Vanessa, let's go home now," Nils whined, pulling on her arm.

"Maybe that's not such a bad idea," Lycra Girl commented, kneeling to tend to her fallen comrade. She looked like she'd rollerbladed right out of a Coors Light commercial.

"Hey." Vanessa was in no mood to take crap from some bimbo stranger. "Next time watch where you're going."

"Vanessa?" Mr. rollerblader-who'd-fallen-on-his-ass demanded, struggling to sit up.

Vanessa's eyelids flapped up and down in disbelief. Was she seeing things?

There, splayed out on the asphalt under the oaks, in the middle of Central Park, wearing rollerblades, dorky athletic shorts, and a clingy white spandex tee, plus wristbands, kneepads, and elbow pads, with a flushed face and messy, sweaty hair, was Dan. Her Dan.

"*Dan?*" she gasped with so much horror and confusion in her voice that Edgar actually stopped blubbering and stood up.

"Hi." Dan grinned sheepishly. The blond bimbo in the skimpy jog bra extended her hand and helped him to his feet. He swiveled unsteadily on his blades. "Hey Vanessa . . . what's up?"

"What's up is she's not paying attention to these little animals running around," the blonde started, tugging her shorts so high she was in grave danger of causing some severe camel toe. "And I'm really trying to be very Zen about this, but—"

"Who *are* you?" Vanessa demanded.

"Who are *you?*" the girl retorted bitchily.

"I'm his *girlfriend,*" Vanessa replied.

Lycra Butt recoiled a little.

"Wait," Vanessa insisted. "What are you *doing?*" She studied Dan critically. His outfit was so completely ridiculous she could barely look at him. She turned back to the girl. "You must be the reason I never see Dan around the house anymore."

"You guys *live* together?"

The words from Dan's poem flooded into Vanessa's head:

Pure love. Pure lust. Trust trust.
Buddha was no Jesus. Neither am I.
I'm just a guy.

"Who are these kids, anyway?" Dan wondered aloud.

"We're her friends," snapped one of the twins—Vanessa still couldn't tell them apart—sticking his tongue out at Dan.

"Your friends?" Dan repeated.

"Right," Vanessa snapped. "Kind of like *she's* your friend, right, Dan?"

A church bell rang down on Fifth Avenue. The sound was

so pure and so totally inappropriate for the moment, it made Vanessa want to scream.

"Vanessa?" The other twin tugged on her hand. "I don't feel so good."

"Not now," Vanessa responded sternly.

"I'm confused," Dan stuttered. "Why aren't you on set right now?"

"I was fired. Not that you'd care."

"Let's just pause before we say anything we're going to regret," interrupted Short Shorts. Pigeons were picking at the sticky remains of the twins' ice creams. If only one of them would peck the bitchy blonde in the ass.

"Vanessa?" the same twin whined. "I *really* don't—" But before he could finish his sentence, he vomited chewed-up ice cream sandwich all over Dan's acid green Nike rollerblades.

So *that's* the definition of bad karma.

he's lost that lovin' feelin'

Nate's legs felt a little shaky, the way they did when Coach caught him goofing off at practice and sentenced him to run laps as punishment. It had been a long day of ferrying new fence posts from the driveway, where they lay piled up higher than he stood, to various points around the yard. He lurched into the house, arms aching and knees wobbling.

Weak in the knees—and not even because of a girl.

On his way to his bedroom he stopped in the bright, white-and-steel kitchen and rummaged in the refrigerator. Regina, his parents' maid/caretaker/chef, kept the place well stocked but Nate pushed aside the terrine of homemade paté and the heirloom-tomato-and-orzo salad to grab a bottle of Lorina orangeade. It had always been his favorite when he was a kid, but for some reason they only ever had it when they were out in East Hampton, so he associated the light, fizzy taste with the carefree summers of his childhood, when he'd hosted outrageous skinny-dipping pool parties and cleaned out his parents' wine cellar.

Those were the days, he thought to himself as he made his way into his bedroom. There'd been nothing to worry about except whether it would be sunny enough to spend the afternoon at the beach, or if he was high enough, or if he'd ever manage to hook up with Blair.

These days life was so much more complicated. Even

though it was summer vacation, Nate was stressed out about a bunch of stuff: what Tawny's townie buddies would do to him if he ever ran into them without Tawny, what he would say to Blair when he saw her at Yale, whether what Chuck Bass had told him about her was true.

Clutching the open bottle, Nate collapsed into his soft, unmade bed with a groan. He closed his eyes and tried to clear his head, but there was one person he couldn't stop picturing.

Guess who?

Suddenly he wished he hadn't returned the moss green cashmere V-neck Blair had given him the spring before last when her dad took them skiing in Sun Valley. He'd put it on, close his eyes, and remember simpler times, when he and Blair were together and all seemed right with the world. Because, except for those times when he'd pissed her off by saying the wrong thing or getting baked and flaking out on plans, being with Blair— however difficult she was—made Nate feel complete, like everything was exactly the way it was supposed to be. Now Blair was going to marry that English guy. Was it really true? Suddenly, Nate had to know.

He sat up, took a swig from the chilly bottle of orangeade and reached for the black Bang & Olufsen telephone on his bedside table. He hesitated for a second before dialing those familiar digits.

"It's Blair." She answered after a couple of rings. She sounded curt, professional, like she hadn't recognized the number.

"Hey." Nate turned over onto his stomach and fiddled nervously with the sheets.

"Nate?" she yawned, sounding bored already. "God, I'm sorry. I'm so *tired*."

"Yeah, it's me," he replied sheepishly. He suddenly couldn't remember why he had thought calling Blair would be a good idea.

"I'm working," Blair explained. "It's been a crazy week."

"That's cool." Blair had a *job*? Wow, things really had changed.

"Yes," she agreed. "Bailey Winter has really been busting my ass."

Nate had no idea what she was talking about but decided he should try to be sympathetic. "That's too bad."

"It's just life in fashion. Where are you, anyway?"

"East Hampton. My parents' place. I'm doing some work for my coach down here, helping him with his house."

"I wish I could get away," Blair replied dreamily. "Just for a minute. But you know what it's like. . . ."

"Yeah," Nate agreed. "If you're working, that's how it goes."

"Did I mention I'm doing wardrobe on that new movie—*Breakfast at Fred's*?"

"Cool," Nate intoned. Why hadn't she said anything about her engagement? "So, you're back from London, I guess."

"Oh, yes." Blair sighed deeply, "I had to get back to New York. I decided this was the best way to build up my résumé before we start Yale, you know, get some real, professional experience under my belt."

"That sounds like a good plan," Nate agreed, suddenly wishing he'd rolled a joint before making the call. "Especially now that you're, you know, making plans for the future."

"Aren't you?" asked Blair. "You've got to think about what lies ahead, you know that, Nate, right?"

"Right," Nate agreed, even though he rarely thought farther ahead than whether to get a burrito or pizza for dinner. "So, anyway, I guess I was just calling to say congratulations, you know."

"Oh, it's nothing. Just a little summer job with one of the best designers in America."

"I was talking about the engagement. I heard everything."

"Engagement?" Blair echoed. "Who have you been talking to?"

"Chuck told me," Nate admitted, pulling a pillow over his head.

"Chuck told you I was engaged?" Blair barked. "As usual, he's got the story all wrong."

"What do you mean?" Nate pulled the pillow off and sat up.

"Well, I'm back," Blair pointed out. "It just wasn't working out in London. I couldn't marry him. I need to think about my future."

Like someone had actually proposed? As if.

"So you're *not* getting married? I should set Chuck straight."

Good luck with that.

"He's an idiot," Blair declared. "Who cares what he thinks? Why would you ever listen to him?"

Nate shrugged, even though Blair couldn't see him over the telephone. "I just didn't know, you know, I hadn't heard from you or anything. But I'm glad you're back. I know it was always your dream to be Katharine Hepburn, but it's cool that at least you get to be close to the action."

"It's *Audrey* Hepburn," Blair corrected him. "And I'm not *close* to the action, I'm an integral part of the action. In a major motion picture like this, wardrobe is critical."

"Remember that time we watched that movie and you kept pausing it and making me practice the lines with you?" Nate reminisced wistfully. It had been a snow day and school was canceled, so they spent the afternoon cuddling in her bed and watching *Breakfast at Tiffany's*, only Blair kept pausing it to recite the lines and trying to convince Nate to go along with it. He'd tried, because it was easier to just keep her happy. Now he was in the Hamptons and Blair was in New York and their relationship was over—even the bedroom was gone, turned into Blair's baby sister's luxurious pastel-colored nursery.

"I've decided that as a long-term career goal, working in fashion, behind the scenes, makes a lot more sense," Blair explained.

"Yeah," Nate agreed. "Serena's the one who's really cut out to be a movie star anyway."

Ouch.

Blair paused for a moment. "I should really get going, Nate. I've got to run some samples uptown to the set."

"Okay." Nate was disappointed. "That sounds important."

"It is important. Have fun at the beach." Blair hung up.

Nate pressed end and dropped the receiver onto the floor, then turned over and stared at the ceiling. *Have fun?* Suddenly, the Hamptons didn't seem fun at all. His whole summer stretched before him and he felt lonely and isolated. He missed the city, he missed his friends, he missed Blair.

And no island babe could ever make him forget that.

v finds a father figure

Slamming the heavy door behind her, Vanessa stormed into the foyer of the Humphrey homestead, dropping her battered army surplus knapsack onto the creaky parquet floor and upsetting a stack of old newspapers in the process.

"Damn!" She knelt and restacked the newspapers as tidily as she could, but the apartment was always in such a state of disarray it hardly seemed to matter.

"What's that?" a booming voice called out. "Who's there?"

Vanessa stood and looked around guiltily. She was so exhausted from her afternoon with the tireless twins, so humiliated and pissed off from her run-in with Dan and his tight-butted rollerblading slut, so furious about getting fired by the psychotic Ken Mogul, that she had forgotten that she wasn't at home: she couldn't just stomp around, slamming doors. She was technically a guest.

"What's all this racket?" Rufus Humphrey shuffled into the dimly lit foyer, clutching a sheaf of loose-leaf papers to his barrel chest. His thick tangle of frizzy gray shoulder-length hair was tied up in a green twist-tie, there were peanut shells in his salt-and-pepper beard, and his glasses had slid all the way down his broad red nose. He was wearing a tattered pair of beige cargo shorts with several pens and highlighters sticking out of one of the pockets, a light blue way-too-tight wine-stained polo that Vanessa recognized as one of Dan's discarded school shirts, and a pink plastic apron embellished with daisies.

"I'm so sorry," Vanessa apologized. "I didn't mean to disturb you."

"What day is this?" Rufus demanded, staring at her intently without any hint of recognition.

She wondered if she should remind him who she was. "Sunday."

"Sunday, yes, Sunday." Rufus nodded, tearing off his rimless reading glasses and tucking them into one of his many pockets. "So, are you home late or early? Should I scold you or something?"

Vanessa laughed, relieved that he seemed to know exactly who she was. "Don't worry. I can assure you I've been behaving."

"Come in, then," he urged, turning and retreating to the steamy and disorderly kitchen. "I've been working on dinner, and I need a fresh palate to sample what I've come up with."

As if she hasn't had a rough enough day already.

Vanessa stationed herself on one of the rickety, uneven chairs at the kitchen table, sipping a glass of murky tap water and watching Rufus Humphrey busy himself at the stove. Whatever he was cooking it was very fragrant and it made her stomach growl noisily. The only thing she'd eaten that day was her hastily scarfed ice cream sandwich; after the whole scene in the park she just hadn't been in the mood for lunch.

"Taste this," Rufus commanded, handing Vanessa a wooden spoon.

She blew on the steaming mound of couscous and sampled it. "Really good."

"It's a tagine," Rufus informed her. "Paul Bowles's recipe. I totally forgot I had it. Where's Dan? He loves Paul Bowles. He'd get a kick out of this, I just know it. I replaced the saffron with vermouth!"

"Dan? I'm not really sure," Vanessa admitted. She fiddled

uncomfortably with the faded white linen place mat, which was embroidered with little lavender flowers. It seemed so out of place in that moldy, disorganized kitchen.

"Trouble in paradise?" Rufus asked, energetically stirring the bubbling pot.

Vanessa hesitated. She was really in the mood to just spill her guts. She hadn't spoken to Ruby since leaving the apartment in a huff, she hadn't talked to her parents in ages. She didn't even care that Rufus was Dan's dad, she just needed to talk to someone.

"Paradise," she scoffed. "I don't think we're living there anymore."

"What do you mean?" Rufus paged through a cookbook, nodding sagely. "Shit! *Two* teaspoons. Well . . . six teaspoons isn't going to kill anyone."

"I mean," explained Vanessa, a lump forming in her throat, "I think we're broken up."

"What happened?" Rufus asked as he rifled through a drawer, clattering the utensils together.

"I don't know," Vanessa lied, suddenly embarrassed. Did he really need to hear all the gory details?

"You kids." He shook his head. "Young love."

Or young love*less*.

Trying not to lose control, Vanessa continued. "And the thing is, he doesn't even know what else is going on in my life. I mean, I lost my job today. I got fired by Ken Mogul." She sighed, her whole body trembling. Hearing the words out loud, even out of her own mouth, made the reality even more harsh.

"Fired?" Rufus repeated, adding what looked like way too much honey to the couscous pot. "Don't worry about it. Believe it or not, I once got fired from a job. I was an usher at the Brattle Theater, back when I was a student." He chuckled. "I got canned for screaming obscenities during a play about red Russia, but it's kind of a long story."

"Well, I really appreciate you letting me stay here. I'm sure

I'll figure out another place to go soon," Vanessa mumbled miserably. "I can call Ruby and maybe she'll let me crash on the couch. Or maybe I can ask Blair Waldorf for help. I mean, I helped her out when she didn't have any place to go."

Miss Sleeps-in-a-new-bed-every-week? Don't count on it, sister.

"Hold the phone, dude!" Rufus exclaimed with one of his classic nonsensical outbursts. "Last I checked, this was my apartment, not Dan's. Jenny's in Europe, and then she's off to that schmancy boarding school. Dan's going to Evergreen, of all places, and I'm gonna be stuck talking to myself and cooking for one. I don't think so, dude."

Vanessa had never been called "dude" before, at least not by someone's dad. She kind of liked it.

"I don't know," she protested. Finally, someone was being *nice* to her, and she had no idea how to handle it. "I'm not sure I'd feel right taking advantage of your hospitality like that."

"If that's really how you feel." Rufus replaced the lid on the cast-iron pot with a bang. "We can work something out. You're going to be at NYU in the fall, right? Not much income there, and you'll be studying too hard to work. Maybe you can rent Jenny's room for a small fee. As long as you promise to let me cook for you."

Vanessa rubbed her stubbly head and blinked up at wild-haired Rufus.

"Ah! Chili powder!" he yelled, before dumping in several tablespoons.

Sure, he was a little weird, but he was really nice and she was sure the rent would be more than reasonable. She could make herself scarce until Dan left for Evergreen. And maybe it would actually be fun rooming with Rufus. He'd be the wacky dad she'd never had. Actually, she did have one, but it couldn't hurt to have two.

"Thank you, Mr. Humphrey." Vanessa wiped her eyes with the backs of her hands. "I'd love to."

"Great. Now grab some bowls and a couple of wineglasses. Supper's on."

Better grab the Pepto while you're at it.

a star is born—take two

Serena cowered inside her trailer for as long as possible, studying her script for the millionth time, trying to soothe her horrible Monday morning jitters. She sipped her second latte of the morning and thought back to her weekend rehearsals with Blair.

"Close your eyes," ordered Kristina, her thin-as-a-wisp German makeup artist. Kristina wore insanely heavy black eyeliner and Serena was slightly terrified of her.

She felt the soft caress of a brush across her closed eyes.

"Okay, open," Kristina said. "All done."

Serena opened her eyes and sighed. At least she didn't have any lines in this big scene, just lyrics: that morning they were shooting a direct reference to the scene in the original film when Audrey Hepburn sings "Moon River" on the fire escape. Ken Mogul had decided to re-create the scene in its entirety, so Serena's trailer was stationed outside of the dilapidated East Village tenement that was her character's home in the movie. Serena downed the last drop of her Starbucks latte and thought about what Blair had told her the day before. She could almost hear Blair's voice inside her head.

Now there's a scary thought.

"You don't have to act. You're already her. *That dress is* your *dress. That voice is* your *voice. Own it."*

"I think they're waiting for you," Kristina reminded her.

Glancing at herself one last time in the bulb-lined vanity, Serena swallowed. She was as ready as she was going to get, but it was going to take a miracle to pull this off.

A miracle named Blair Waldorf.

She stepped out of her gleaming chrome Airstream trailer and onto the sidewalk. St. Marks Place felt even more claustrophobic than usual: it was crowded with an army of crew members and a forest of incredibly hot lights. Ken Mogul was slumped in his usual canvas director's chair, smoking a cigarette, since they were shooting in the open air and not the pristine environs of Barneys, and fiddling with his new BlackBerry.

Blair waited between the two trailers with her loyal shadow/assistant Jasmine. The younger girl had a long Kelly green garment bag stamped with the ornate logo of the designer Bailey Winter tossed over her shoulder, ready to protect Serena's gown from the elements when the scene was over.

It must be nice to have a sherpa.

"Serena on set!" called the second assistant director, and Ken's army of crew began to dash around like ants.

As soon as he noticed his leading lady, Ken Mogul leapt out of his seat, almost colliding with a four-eyed intern. Behind the director, Serena could see the chiseled profile of Thaddeus Smith, leaning against his own trailer—a vintage Airstream identical to hers, only painted baby blue—chattering into a tiny black cell phone.

"Holly, love," cooed Ken, tucking his BlackBerry into the back pocket of his weirdly inappropriate tuxedo pants. "You look ravishing. The costume is absolutely flawless."

Serena was wearing Bailey Winter's night-blue velvet smock dress and the prettiest silver bow-tie flats. Of course her legs were long and perfect, not that she ever exercised.

Exercise? How gauche.

"Thanks," Serena replied shakily. She couldn't wait get this over with.

"Good," Ken barked. "Let's get some light in here! This is the real thing, people!"

Serena strolled over to her mark on the set, just as she'd practiced walking yesterday.

"Let's get light," called the assistant director.

The light changed: the rest of the room grew darker but the spot on Serena was intensely bright. She didn't even blink. She looked up into the light and she couldn't see anything but the light, and couldn't think about anything but standing there in the light. She was Serena. She was Holly. She didn't know who she was anymore. She just *was*.

Own it, she reminded herself.

"Whenever you're ready, Holly," Ken called from somewhere out in the darkness.

She was ready.

Taking a deep breath, she walked to the bottom step of the tenement's stoop. She didn't hesitate, she didn't count her steps, she didn't stumble or run. Mounting the steps, she turned to face the cameras, inhaling deeply.

"It's a nice night," she sighed. "It's always a nice night."

She climbed to the top step and sat down. She could see Ken Mogul watching her intently as he puffed on a cigarette. She could see Blair, standing very still and squinting critically. She paused and then, with a heartbreaking little tremor in her voice, she began to sing.

Moon River, wider than a mile . . .
I'll be crossing you in style, someday.
Dream maker, you heartbreaker . . .

She sang through all the verses of the song, unaccompanied. The set was completely quiet and the light so strong she forgot for a moment who she really was, where she really was: for the moment, she *was* Holly, and she was singing her heart out.

She finished the song and a tiny tear rolled down her

cheek. She stared into the light, blinking and half smiling. She'd always been the center of attention; in fact, she was so used to it she barely noticed anymore. But this was the first time she'd ever felt like a star.

There was a long moment of complete and utter silence. No one moved. No one spoke.

"Holly," whispered Ken quietly, but everyone could hear him—it was that quiet. "That was incredible. Where the *fuck* have you been keeping that, sweetheart?" He leapt out of his chair and dashed onto the set to scoop her up in his arms. Some of the crew actually started clapping. Even Blair.

"Ladies and gentlemen!" Ken Mogul cried, holding Serena closely against his chest and spinning her around in a circle. "A star is born!"

Ken smelled like sauerkraut and espresso. It made her eyes tear. But that was okay—she was already crying.

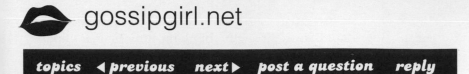
Disclaimer: All the real names of places, people, and events have been altered or abbreviated to protect the innocent. Namely, me.

hey people!

So I happened to be walking by Barneys the other day (okay, I admit it: I've been keeping a vigil) and guess what? It was open. That's right: up and running, back to normal, and not a moment too soon. I scooped up some adorable Margiela drawstring pants that will do quite nicely poolside and headed upstairs to Fred's, which has been restored to its normal glory. I guess it's true what I've been hearing: filming on that movie has wrapped. Wonder how our favorite leading lady did? Reports from the set have it that (surprise, surprise) she pulled through quite nicely (that's our girl!), nailing every take so precisely even her famously sourpuss director couldn't stop smiling and declaring his love for her. Take a number, buddy. The even better news is, as any Hollywood player will tell you, that the end of filming means one thing: the wrap party. I hear this one is going to be a complete old-school blowout, so cross your fingers and check with your doorman every hour on the hour to see if the invitation has arrived. Mine, of course, arrived days ago.

a public service announcement

We interrupt this program to inform you of a very important development: ABC Carpet & Home, the only place in Manhattan where you'll find handwoven rugs from Iran and those so-delicious-smelling-you-want-to-eat-them Diptyque candles under one roof, is now offering a special service to its devoted customers. Stop by and ask for Sisi; she'll help you pick out a glorious feather bed (because those university-issue mattresses are paper thin), a charming Turkish kilim (the better to cover up the dreary cinder-block walls), a nice chandelier (go for vintage, one-of-a-kind ones to counteract the—shudder—dorm room fluorescents), and all the little odds and ends that make a house (even a teensy dorm room) into a home. You know, it's never too soon to start prepping for fall!

your e-mail

Dear GG,
I was picnicking on the Hudson last weekend and I swear I saw a certain Hollywood stud rollerblading shirtless by the river. I'd recognize that chiseled jaw and those even more chiseled abs anywhere. Could it really be? Because here's the thing: he was wearing these teeny spandex shorts that showed off his taut little butt and underneath his skates I'm pretty sure I caught a glimpse of some rainbow socks. What gives? Please don't say what I think you're going to say.
—ThadRulz

Dear ThadRulz,
When did rollerblading become so popular again? That really snuck up on me. Anyway, all I'll say is this: straight boys are allowed to rollerblade too. In fact, I can think of one (definitely straight arrow) who has recently discovered his love of the sport. If you're looking for evidence that **T** prefers the company of gentlemen, some say he's had affairs with everyone from a certain director's considerably younger wife to the director himself. You can't believe everything you read . . . unless you read it here!
—GG

Dear GG,
I'm in a rough spot. I've got this totally adorable neighbor who I thought I really hit it off with. All good, right? Well,

then her just-as-adorable roommate moved in, and I think
I might have hit it off even better with her. What do you
think? Should I attempt the roommate swap, or am I better
off dating outside my zip code?
—Indecision

Dear Indecision,
You're a brave fellow. Just make sure the love affair lasts
as long as the lease—otherwise you're in for some
uncomfortable moments in the stairwell! And hey, there's
nothing more fun than a threesome!
—GG

sightings

N looking moony on a bench on Main Street in East Hampton.
Wonder what has him down? **D** and an unidentified girl at
Jamba Juice in Columbus Circle, "replenishing their fluids" after
a tough workout. Hey kids, you do know there are, like, four
hotels nearby, don't you? **B** schlepping some tightly packed garment bags to her mother's place on Fifth Avenue. Hasn't she
bought enough this summer? Or is keeping the leftovers just a
fringe benefit of her new career in fashion? **T** buying flowers at
Chelsea Market—just a little token for his favorite leading lady?
V toting her collected works to the Fifth Avenue mansion where
she's working now. It seems that her new boss is quite a film
buff, or maybe she's just trying to get fired again by showing
her charges some really twisted stuff.

Okay, that's enough with the sightings. I don't have time for this,
really; I'm on my way to that amazing vintage boutique on
Elizabeth Street. I don't usually go for old clothes— they smell
like dead people—but I thought it might be fun to dress the old-
school Hollywood part for the old-school Hollywood party.
Oops, I've already said too much!

You know you love me.

gossip girl

a real hollywood ending

The rooftop bar at the Oceana Hotel was a madhouse. It was crowded on any given summer night, but throw a couple of movie stars into the mix (okay, one movie star and one soon-to-be movie star) and it was chaos. The open-air rooftop bar and pool was more a place to see and be seen rather than a place to talk and be heard, so Serena was a little disappointed when Thaddeus suggested it. Now that the pressure of filming was off her shoulders, Serena wanted to really talk to him, to get to know him as a person, not a costar. She'd heard a rumor that he was going to be leaving town after the wrap party, which was tomorrow, so that didn't leave them with much time together—and she hoped that something might finally happen between them, off-camera.

Apparently that was the *only* rumor she'd heard about him.

"What are you drinking?" Thaddeus shouted when their waitress approached to take their order. They were seated in what was supposedly the VIP section, but there was nothing to distinguish it from the rest of the narrow terrace, except for the fact that they had the best, most unobstructed view of the Hudson. At least they'd chosen the right night to drink by the river. Fireworks were going off all over, in celebration of something or other. Gay Pride, maybe? Or maybe there was a marathon today. Serena could never keep things like that straight.

"Caipirinha," she practically shouted into his ear.

Thaddeus repeated this to the starstruck waitress, who hurried off to fetch the drinks that would probably be on the house. Thaddeus never had to pay for anything, but then again, Serena had never really had to pay for anything either: The notorious fashion designer Les Best had given her a ton of clothes when she modeled for his perfume ad, and guys were always buying her drinks or picking up dinner no matter where she went.

Guess stardom was in her stars.

Thaddeus idly drummed on the surface of the table in time with the Scissor Sisters tune that was blaring out of the cleverly hidden speakers. He stared out over the Hudson and smiled.

"It's a great night," he observed.

"It is," Serena agreed. She was squeezed in between Thaddeus and the protective railing that snaked around the terrace. "I'm so glad we get to be out and not have to worry about going over our lines or what Ken's going to yell at us tomorrow."

"Fucking tell me about it." Thaddeus lit a cigarette, took a quick drag, and then passed it off to Serena.

Serena inhaled the slightly damp butt—she'd already made out with Thaddeus on camera, so a bit of his spit didn't bother her—as the waitress set down their drinks. Thaddeus slid her cocktail across the table to her. "A toast," he suggested, lifting his pink cosmo into the air.

Pink cosmo?

"Definitely." Serena clinked her glass to his. "To an incredible movie."

"To an incredible costar," Thaddeus corrected, cocking his eyebrow. "And an incredible debut."

He draped his arm over the back of the bench and pulled Serena a little closer, resting his left hand on her left shoulder. "The fireworks are going to really get going soon, huh?" He nodded toward the river, where a small one had already exploded.

The DJ started playing a mellower tune, something by the Raves.

"I know this song!" Serena cried. It sounded familiar but she couldn't place it.

"It's the Raves," Thaddeus explained. "I'm pretty tight with their drummer." He reached over and took the burning cigarette from Serena, inhaling furtively.

"Really? I know the girl singing. Her name's Jenny. We went to high school together. Wait, I think she might have dated your friend, the drummer, what's his name . . . ?"

"No." Thaddeus laughed. "I don't think she's quite his type."

Oh? And what type is that?

Serena wasn't sure what that was supposed to mean, but she hadn't come there to discuss Jenny Humphrey's romantic life. She sipped her sugary drink and batted her eyelashes at the crowd of girls that had assembled just beyond the velvet rope bordering the VIP area. The girls, all boasting hideous blowouts and way too much eyeliner, were giggling and taking pictures of her and Thaddeus with their cell phones.

They're probably going to e-mail them to some gossip Web site, thought Serena with annoyance.

Oh, don't be such a ninny.

A massive round of fireworks erupted with a violent bang, and Serena gave a frightened little yelp, burying herself in Thaddeus Smith's warm, muscular embrace.

"Don't worry." He laughed. "It's just noise."

"I think our cover is blown," Serena told him, gesturing with her eyes toward the gaggle of girls.

"I'll never quite get used to it." Thaddeus frowned. "I mean, no doubt some fuzzy little camera phone picture of us will end up in the papers."

"Yeah, it's weird," Serena whispered, accidentally grazing Thaddeus's ear with the tip of her nose.

"Do me a favor?" Thaddeus asked.

Before Serena could open her mouth to answer, he leaned in and kissed her gently on the lips. The timing was perfect: over the Hudson a massive explosion of fireworks resounded with a bang, their lights twinkling and then fading in an instant. It was totally cheesy but totally romantic: a totally Hollywood moment.

Like, *whoa.*

n's woman trouble

"Dude! Nate!" Anthony Avuldsen leaned out the window of his black BMW M3, honking the horn.

Nate was locking his bike to a PRIVATE PROPERTY, NO TRESPASSING sign on the edge of Main Beach's dirt parking lot. He was supposed to meet Tawny but Anthony's appearance was a welcome surprise. After talking to Blair on the phone . . . he just couldn't help but feel like he was with the wrong girl. Plus, he was about twenty minutes early.

There's a first time for everything.

"Hey," Nate called, strolling over to the driver's side of the car. "What's going on?"

"Not much." Anthony grinned. "I was just on my way home from the beach, but why don't you get in and we'll go for a ride?" He reached into the car's ashtray and plucked out a freshly rolled joint, waving it in the air. "Just a quick drive, you know?"

That was all the invitation Nate needed. He walked around the car and hopped into the passenger side, settling into the soft, cream-colored leather seat.

Anthony turned down the stereo and pressed a button so that Nate's window lowered quickly. He circled the car around the parking lot and out onto the street. "Go ahead and start it up," he urged.

Nate grabbed the joint, pulled his trusty Bic from his sock, and lit it.

"Good time the other night at Isabel's." Anthony reached over to take the joint from Nate. "Sorry you couldn't make it."

Nate exhaled a long plume of smoke out the window. He studied his reflection in the windshield: he hadn't had time to shave that morning and was looking kind of stubbly. His T-shirt was filthy and his deodorant had given out hours ago: his jeans were grass-stained and dingy. He was sporting an incredible tan but still looked a bit unhealthy, probably because he hadn't been sleeping much, and his eyes were a little bloodshot.

Is lack of sleep really the culprit here?

He turned to take the joint back from Anthony and studied his friend more closely: Anthony was wearing a pair of crazy printed Vilebrequin board shorts, some beat-up old flip-flops, and a pair of sunglasses. He had a tan to rival Nate's but no bags under his crystal-clear eyes and he looked like a million other guys in the Hamptons: like a guy on vacation, driving home from the beach, having a quick smoke. Nate exhaled unhappily. The pot was great but it didn't change the fact that he was tired, he was bummed out, he was . . . jealous. Why did Anthony get to chill at the beach all day while he had to work like a dog?

Maybe because Anthony didn't steal performance-enhancing drugs from his lax coach?

Nate drummed on the windowsill in time with the old Dylan disc on the stereo and drifted off for a moment, imagining the ideal summer: he'd be at the beach, of course, surfing at Montauk or just lazing around on the sand, tooling around in his dad's Aston Martin convertible, smoking with Anthony and his other friends from the lacrosse team, staying in bed with Blair until the early afternoon. Or maybe he'd take Blair sailing for a couple of weeks along the coast of Maine. Teach her how to fish. Eat lobster. Have lots of sex. Sleep. Have more sex. Go for a swim. Sex again.

"Dude, you there?" Anthony asked.

"Sorry," Nate mumbled, coming back to reality.

"It's cool." Anthony pulled up to a red light. Three girls sauntered by in bikini tops and surf shorts. They were only about thirteen but they were still cute. "So what's the deal with that Tawny chick, man? She's hot."

"Yeah," Nate replied, passing the joint back. "She's cool. I don't know, though. Maybe I'm off girls right now or something."

Anthony burst out laughing, choking a little on the joint. "Right, right. I've heard that before."

"Shit, man," Nate clarified. "She's just no Blair, you know what I mean?"

"Well, there's only one Blair," replied Anthony in his stoner drawl, stubbing out the roach in the car's built-in ashtray. He ran his hand through his beach-blond shag of hair. "So, you two getting back together?"

Nate shook his head miserably. He was stuck with life as an indentured servant. Blair was busy being a fashion maven. He'd been so stupid, always fucking everything up with her, always taking her for granted or mistakenly hooking up with her best friend or whatever, that he'd been blind to the reality that without Blair his life was nothing.

Looks like Blair isn't the only drama queen.

back to the scene of the crime

Serena crept up the creaky metal steps to her trailer quietly—or as quietly as was possible in her clunky metallic silver Michael Kors wedges. She wasn't even supposed to be there; the actors had all been released from their duties and the only people around were the crew responsible for striking the set. But Serena had decided to tag along with Blair that Wednesday—she wanted to grab the tiny black dress that Bailey Winter had designed for her to wear, as Holly, in the climactic party scene in the movie. It was the perfect thing to wear to her *real* party the next night.

Stepping into the trailer, Serena switched on the light and closed the flimsy door behind her. The vanity was still littered with makeup and hair supplies, and all of her costumes, lovingly labeled and steamed to perfection by Blair's stalker/intern, were hung, an inch apart, on a rolling rack.

Gotcha. Serena grabbed the perfect little black dress. It was cut to fit her proportions exactly, and though the thin shoulder straps were covered with a subtle spray of jet-black beading, it was otherwise sleek and simple. This was so much easier than shopping.

Right, shopping is a total drag.

Tearing open the plastic cover that kept the dust at bay, Serena slipped the dress off its hanger and wadded it up into her bag. Technically, she wasn't supposed to just help herself to the costumes. Stealing it out of the trailer gave her a rush she'd only experienced one other time, when she was ten and stole a Bonne Belle bubblegum Lip Smacker from Boyd's. A knock on the trailer door made her freeze, petrified.

"Who is it?" she asked shakily, quickly zipping up her orange Hermès canvas tote.

"Thad?" A thin, gorgeously tanned guy poked his head through the trailer door. His spiky brown hair was in artful disarray, and beneath his perfectly arched eyebrows his eyes were huge and green, with long, beautiful lashes. He wore a snug black sleeveless tee and sported intricate tattoos of fish up and down his long, skinny arms.

"No, it's me," Serena apologized. "Thad's trailer is the next one over."

"Oh my gosh!" The boy blushed deeply. "I'm *so* sorry. I guess I should know better than to go charging into trailers."

"No, no, it's okay." Serena relaxed when she realized he wasn't there to bust her for stealing. "I'm Serena."

"Oh my gosh, hi!" the stranger cried, skipping into the trailer, wallet chain jingling, hands extended, letting the door slam behind him.

So much for stealing clothes in the still of the night.

"Oh my gosh, *Serena*. It's so good to meet you finally." He grabbed her free hand in both of his and held it.

"Um, you too," she stammered. He had the faintest accent that she couldn't quite place and she was drawing a total blank. Was she supposed to know this guy?

"Damn, would you look at me? Just barging in here? You're in the middle of something and I just swoop in like any gushing fan off the street. I'm so sorry. You must think I'm crazy." The boy released her hand and shook his head, laughing.

"No, no, I'm not busy or anything," she lied, clutching her tote close to her chest. "I was just picking up something I left behind."

"So Thad said you guys are all done shooting?" the boy

asked. "Do you mind if I sit? I'm gonna sit." He settled into the chair in front of the vanity and crossed his legs.

Please sit.

"Yeah, we're done. Thank God!" Serena tried not to look as perplexed as she felt. Who *was* this guy?

"It's crazy work, but somebody's got to do it." He recrossed his legs and leaned back, studying her from head to toe. "But you look fabulous. Gorgeous. Just like Thad said."

"Right. Thad," she repeated, growing suspicious.

"Oh my gosh, I totally didn't introduce myself. I have a tendency to do that. I just talk and talk, because I get nervous usually, although you're so sweet and pretty I don't see how you could make anyone nervous, unless it was some boy who wanted to ask you out. . . ."

Serena blushed. Who was this person?

"And I'm still babbling," he continued. "Oh my gosh, I'm so stupid sometimes. I'm Serge. It's so great to meet you finally."

"Serge," she repeated. *Serge? Serge? Who the hell was Serge?*

"Serge. Thad's boyfriend?" he clarified. "I can't believe it's been so long and we haven't met before now. I'll have to punch Thad when I see him. Keeping us apart like this. Ridiculous."

Thad's . . . *what?*

"Oh, Thad talks about you so much," she lied. "I can't believe that we never met either."

"I guess it *kind* of makes sense," Serge admitted, grabbing a tub of concealer off the vanity and fiddling with it. "We've got to be kind of discreet, so most of the time I'm just sitting around my room. I mean, we're not even in the same *hotel*. I'm holed up at the Mercer. But you know how it is—you've been posing with those photos with him all around town. You're the sweetest. We both really appreciate it."

Those photos? The kiss had been just for photographers? Thad had been using her? Serena slumped against the wall.

She couldn't believe she'd been so mistaken. She'd thought they'd had a real connection, but he was just a beautiful gay guy with an adorable boyfriend he had to keep secret. She had to sit down.

"Yeah." Serena dropped her bag on the ground and took a seat on the built-in sofa, kicking off her wedges and curling her legs up underneath her. "Well, you know, Thad's the greatest. I'm just happy to help out." She sighed. It was almost the truth. She should have been annoyed or mad or hurt or something, but really, she couldn't believe she hadn't figured it out sooner.

Not that she'd gotten too many clues.

"I told him he was so lucky to be working with such an awesome costar. I mean, sometimes his leading ladies get so crazy and possessive they actually think they're *dating*. It's like they can't tell the difference between fantasy and reality. I mean, hello? It's just *pretend*."

"Mmm." Serena nodded.

"But not you," Serge gushed. "You're like an old pro, even though this is your first movie! I want you to be in all of Thad's movies from now on. Promise you will!"

"Oh, stop." Serena giggled. It was hard to be upset or hurt when both Thaddeus and his boyfriend were so *nice*.

"No, I mean it," Serge cried, leaping out of his seat and throwing himself onto the couch next to her. "You *have* to come to our place in Palm Springs for the weekend. We'll have such a ball! And if you're interested . . . I think I might know an awesome guy for you."

"Oh, really?" That sounded fun.

And she could definitely trust his taste in men!

 gossipgirl.net

topics ◀ *previous* *next*▶ *post a question* *reply*

Disclaimer: All the real names of places, people, and events have been altered or abbreviated to protect the innocent. Namely, me.

hey people!

I have literally five minutes to write this—I don't know when summer vacation got so hectic, but between tennis lessons at Ocean Colony and cocktail hour on the roof of the Met, I just don't know where the day goes. Let's start with your e-mail, because there's only one subject on everyone's mind lately. . . .

 Dear GG,
Do you know how I can get an invite to the big party that's coming this Thursday? My boyfriend claims to be taking me, but I suspect he's bluffing and at the last minute his Jeep will break down or something. But I really, really want to go, so I need a plan **B**. Help!
—*Struck

 Dear *Struck,
The word is they're watching the guest list pretty closely. So hopefully your man isn't bluffing—or you're going to be stuck watching the limos arrive like just another commoner. Sorry!
—GG

 Dear GG,
I was just in Amsterdam with my family and managed to sneak away to check out the real sights. After smoking some hash in a coffee shop, I swear I saw that girl **J** dancing in a window in the red light district. Now I wish I'd asked for a lap dance. Tell me it was her!
—Despr8

A: Dear Despr8,
Sorry. Her parents might be alternative, but I'm afraid our **J** isn't. She's off studying fine art and maybe the fine art of fine boys, but lap dancing in the red light district and skeezy tourists are not part of the curriculum.
—GG

perfect your party small talk

A handy refresher course for all my fellow revelers. Enjoy!

1) You're cornered by a lecherous, badly dressed aspiring director who wants you to come back to his place for a private audition. Your response:

a) Dream on, perv.

b) Why go to your place? Grab your video phone and meet me in the bathroom!

c) I'd be happy to, Mr. Mogul.

2) While in the bathroom line, a portly, producer-type-fellow asks what you thought of his movie. Your response:

a) I thought there were some casting problems—for example, the young ingenue could've had more ingenuity—but it wasn't bad. . . .

b) The costumes were pretty, although my belief has always been that when it comes to costumes, less is more.

c) Have you started casting the sequel yet?

3) A world-famous, unbelievably handsome, internationally recognizable movie star asks you to tango. Your response:

a) Tango? I'd rather go somewhere quiet, far from all these paparazzi.

b) Hold me close. Please, just hold me close.

c) I've always found that gay guys make the best dancers!

4) Some leggy starlet type trips and spills her fruity cocktail all over your new taupe suede Sigerson Morrison ballet flats. Your response:

a) Nothing—you just hurl your drink in her face.

b) My shoes! My pride and joy! My raison d'être!

c) Screw it. I'll dance barefoot!

Done yet? Don't cheat.

Okay, the answer to each one is C. Like you didn't know that. See you tonight!

You know you love me.

gossip girl

d's got a golden ticket

Dan had seen Bree in several variations of exercise gear and, of course, completely naked, but he'd never seen her all put together for an evening out. So when he emerged from the 6 train station at Seventy-seventh Street he was taken aback to find her waiting for him, a vision in a simple white silk camisole, with her blond hair—which he'd never seen down—cascading over her sun-kissed shoulders. Her long, below-the-knee embroidered turquoise skirt looked like something she'd unearthed at a flea market in Turkey.

Dan was wearing the closest thing he had to a party outfit: a sharp charcoal gray slim-cut Agnès B. suit, a gift from his former agent, back when he'd been poised to be the literary world's next big thing.

Not a fickle almost-college-dropout who cheats on his live-in girlfriend.

"Hey beautiful," he called boldly, springing off the last step and onto the sidewalk. Taking the steps *was* easier since he'd started his exercise regimen.

"Thanks." Bree kissed his cheek. "Feeling centered? You look good. I hope I'm not underdressed."

"No, you're just right. Should we go?"

They strolled down Lexington amid clouds of bus exhaust. The early evening light shimmered on the windows of Starbucks.

"So." Bree wrapped her arms around herself as she walked. "I'm still not sure I understand why you were invited to this party."

"I'm not sure," Dan admitted. "I know Serena from way back. . . . Or maybe Vanessa put me on the list? Who cares? Party's a party, right?" They turned onto Seventy-first Street.

"That's true." Bree nodded stiffly. She looked a little nervous and uptight for someone who was usually so Zen. "Speaking of Vanessa . . ."

"Right." Dan dug instinctively into his pockets for his Camels.

Too bad he forgot his wheatgrass-and-ginseng cigarettes.

Bree sighed. "I think maybe you need to think this through. Meditate. Breathe deeply. Center yourself. Eventually you'll find clarity. I can't tell you what to do, you know. It's your life. But I'd like to see you find some answers. That's all we want in life, after all, isn't it?"

"Sure, right," Dan mumbled, looking both ways before they crossed Third Avenue. Maybe a taxi would just plow him down and he wouldn't have to have this conversation.

"I don't know." Bree sighed, absentmindedly braiding her hair over one shoulder. "I'm going to Santa Cruz at the end of the summer anyway. I have no claim on you. But we've had a great time, haven't we?"

"Sure. It's been amazing." He paused. "Do you hear that?"

A dull roar broke the evening's quiet: the sound of honking horns and idling cars mixed with the occasional scream and the relentless clicks of a thousand cameras.

"Is that the party?" Bree remarked. "It's so . . . *noisy.*"

Did she expect the party of the month to be a quiet affair?

"Come on," Dan urged, grabbing her hand, thrilled he had an excuse to cut the conversation short. He was not in the mood to discuss the state of his relationship with Vanessa. And the truth was, he had no answers. "I don't want to be late."

Holly Golightly's quiet street was quiet no more. There

were barricades and bouncers stationed at both ends of the block, and an honest-to-God red carpet right down the middle of the street and up to the town house. On Second Avenue, the line of limos was two blocks long, and on the corner was a roped off area heaving with reporters and photographers.

At the door of the town house, Dan surrendered his invite to the massive goateed bouncer, who nodded gruffly and stamped their hands much more forcefully than was necessary.

"Want something to drink?" Dan asked Bree as they strolled past a long table set with elegant champagne flutes.

"I'm not sure I should be drinking tonight," Bree replied in such a stern tone that Dan couldn't help but think she was implying that *he* shouldn't drink either.

Well, isn't she the life of the party?

Dan grabbed two glasses—if she wasn't going to drink, then he could drink for two—and downed one immediately. Burping quietly, he dropped the empty glass on the table and wound his way through the thick crowd, one hand clutching Bree's, the other his chilled champagne. They pushed through the crowd and stepped into the foyer. Bree bounded through the foyer and up the stairs ahead of him. Maybe she was getting into the idea of this party?

"This is great exercise," she observed.

"Yeah, great," Dan agreed, panting along behind her.

As they climbed higher, the din of squealing girls and thumping bass grew louder. The crumbly walls of the town house were surprisingly solid, but even they couldn't contain the racket. When they reached the fourth-floor landing, they ran into the overspill from the apartment above: leering at them from the next floor, the final landing, was the disturbingly groomed Chuck Bass, pet snow monkey perched on his shoulder wearing a pink tutu and brandishing a glistening silver magic wand.

"Romeo!" Chuck called down to Dan in a girly falsetto.

Dan nodded at Chuck hospitably. He loathed that asshole and his freaky vintage eighties mint green Prada zipper suit. He took Bree's hand and pulled her up the steps behind him: it would take some maneuvering to get her safely past Chuck.

"Who's that?" Bree wanted to know.

"No one," Dan told her firmly. They hurried up to the top landing, dodging bodies and bulldozing past Chuck Bass, until they nearly collided with Vanessa. Again.

They *had* to stop meeting like this.

Vanessa was accompanied by the same little boys she'd had in tow in Central Park a couple of days before, only instead of being smeared with ice cream, the kids were all cleaned up, sporting snazzy blue blazers with brass buttons, seersucker shorts, and perfectly pressed white cotton oxfords. Their blond hair was parted in slick, tidy hairstyles. They looked miserable.

"Dan," Vanessa stammered, clearly surprised. "What are you doing here?"

"I . . . I thought maybe you put me on a list . . . before . . ." he stammered. "I didn't think you'd be here, after, you know—"

"Their sister worked on the movie." Vanessa put her hands on top of the boys' heads. "So I had to."

"Hi," said Bree uncomfortably. "I'm Bree. We sort of met the other day."

"I'm Vanessa." She smirked. Bree? What kind of bullshit name was *that*?

"I'm Edgar," offered one of the twins, puffing his chest out proudly. He removed his hand from Vanessa's and extended it in Bree's direction. Maybe he'd forgotten his little puking episode?

"I'm Nils," said the other boy, gently pushing his brother out of the way and beaming at Bree. Dan couldn't help noticing they sounded a little like mini Chucks.

They start early, those Upper East Side boys.

Bree knelt down and looked at the two little boys intensely. "You guys have really clear auras."

Vanessa snickered. Dan cocked his head and studied her. She was basically the same: shaved head, lots of attitude, but instead of her usual black jeans, she was wearing fancy-looking shiny black trousers and instead of a black cotton tank she was wearing a semi-sheer black top that was soft and delicate—it might even have been silk. She looked almost feminine, and although it sounded strange, sometimes Dan forgot she was just that: a girl.

"Want to go somewhere and talk?" he asked tentatively

Vanessa shrugged. "If you can tear yourself away." Bree had the boys in her lap and was reading their palms.

"We kind of have a lot to talk about, don't we?" Dan allowed. Bree began to chant in Sanskrit.

That's the understatement of the year.

all the world's a stage

Because the apartment didn't have any real furniture to speak of, the drunken crowd had turned the large main room into an impromptu dance floor. Blair had downed three Bellinis, so she was ready to answer the call of duty and dance her cute little ass off. Besides, she'd memorized the party scene in *Breakfast at Tiffany's* and knew what was expected of her. Sure, Serena was Holly—there was no denying that at this point—but that didn't mean that she couldn't have a great fucking time, too. She had plenty of booze and the party of her dreams at her disposal.

Not to mention a hot guy.

"Hey," Jason murmured in her ear. "It's good to see you again."

She shimmied a perfect imitation of one of the partygoers from the original movie's big party—but only a true expert like her would recognize that bit of choreography. Her flapper-inspired Blumarine dress moved sexily in time with her body's gyrations, and she clutched an old-fashioned mother-of-pearl cigarette holder in her hand. The only touch she'd decided to skip was the diamond tiara.

She didn't need the headgear to play the part of a princess.

"Dance!" she commanded, grabbing hold of Jason's long, smooth fingers and pulling him closer to her. He had the nicest, wide-open smile she'd ever seen and was so tall and clean looking.

"Yes, ma'am!" He unbuttoned the top button of his light blue Steven Alan oxford. His near-dorkiness was such a turn-on!

Blair drew closer to him, enjoying the way his tremendous height made her feel tiny and delicate and sexy.

Like a certain moon-eyed Hollywood waif?

She could smell the soap on his skin and the beer on his breath, and the rest of the crowd receded into the background as she gazed up at his bright smile dreamily. In that moment, it was hard to remember that she'd ever liked anyone else, including Lord Whateverhisnamewas or Sir Stoner.

"So, you know . . ." Blair batted her eyelashes suggestively. "Serena's heading back to her parents' apartment for the rest of the summer, but I think I might stay here. . . ."

"We'll be neighbors." He smiled. "That could get us in trouble."

"I kind of like trouble."

Hello, understatement.

"Well then . . ." Jason grinned. He bent down and kissed her slowly. His lips were the flavor of the sweet ale he'd been drinking all night and something pepperminty. He was delicious. It was a perfect, *perfect* first kiss.

Afterwards she smiled back at Jason before surveying the room. She was slow dancing with him even though everyone else was jumping and spinning to the upbeat Madonna the DJ had just put on. Blair pulled Jason's warm body even closer, despite the fact that it was basically a hundred and ten degrees inside the overcrowded apartment. And then, out of the corner of her eye, she saw Sir Stoner himself. Fucking fuck. Even now, she could still count on Nate to ruin a perfect moment.

Nate Archibald was hand in hand with someone Blair definitely did not recognize, and not one of those slutty, Marni-clad L'École girls, either. This girl was definitely *not* wearing Marni but rather . . . Target.

Everything about this girl was exaggerated—her tan, her boobs, her lips, her makeup. It all looked fake. Worse than her overteased hair and ridiculous orange-bronzed skin was her outfit: she was wearing peach-colored capri pants and a sequin-encrusted tank top and had accessorized her party ensemble with dirty espadrilles and a bought-on-a-street-corner fake peach satin Prada backpack. She looked like nothing Blair had ever seen. She was a disaster. Blair glanced at Bailey Winter standing on the other side of the room. She'd have paid money to hear what he was whispering to Graham Oliver just then.

"Something wrong?" asked Jason, nuzzling at her neck.

"I'm sorry," she muttered pulling out of his embrace. "I just need a minute."

It takes more than a minute to get over seeing your first love with someone else, though.

what up, roomie?

"Are you okay?" Vanessa asked, because Dan had been quiet too long and was starting to creep her out. "Let's sit." She gestured toward the windowsill behind them. The window overlooked the backyard and was open a bit, admitting a gentle evening breeze. Down in the back garden a group was huddled around a forlorn lilac bush, smoking.

"Things have really changed since graduation, huh?" Dan reached out but put his hand down before actually touching her. "I don't know what's happened this past couple of weeks."

Cut off my fingers. I can't feel anymore.

Can't feel you. Or you. You.

"I guess what's happened," Vanessa began, sternly but not unkindly, "is that you've met someone else. It's okay. I mean, I'm hurt, I guess. But mostly I wish you hadn't tried to keep it from me, especially after you made that scene at Blair's graduation party about staying with me this fall—"

"Scene?" Dan repeated. "I made a scene?" He'd talked to her privately, in a corner. There'd been no *scene*. Okay, his graduation speech had been a scene, but thankfully she'd missed it.

"Anyway that's not the point. The point is," Vanessa continued, "I haven't been completely honest either."

A facially unattractive drunk girl whom Vanessa remembered

was an extra on the movie stumbled up the stairs. She was wearing a cherry red TEAM JOLIE T-shirt and a million silver bangles up her wrist. She glanced at Vanessa but pretended not to recognize her. Being at this party was definitely not Vanessa's idea of a good time.

Party pooper.

"You're seeing someone?" Dan looked like he was going to cry.

"No, of course not." She swatted at the air in front of her. "But I have some weird news: Your dad said I could rent a room from him . . . even though we're broken up. . . ."

Dan winced and rubbed the sole of his shoe against his ankle. He hadn't really thought they were officially broken up, but he guessed they were now. "And?" he asked.

"And I said I wanted to." Vanessa looked at Dan, to see if she could read him, but he was still rubbing his shoe against his leg like a dog with an itch. "I mean, I can't really afford much, and he said he'd give me a really good deal, so . . ."

"Well," Dan said after a moment. "I don't think it'll be weird."

It won't?

"I think it'll be fun," he continued.

It *will*?

"So, friends?" he asked.

"Friends," Vanessa confirmed.

Friends . . . ?

look what the cat dragged in—and who he brought with him

Thaddeus Smith downed his icy caipirinha and leaned toward Serena, whispering sexily, his breath scented with the spicy rum.

"Who is *that*?" he asked.

He didn't point but there was no need to: anyone would know exactly who Thaddeus Smith was talking about. Nate Archibald had arrived.

They were huddled together in the minuscule kitchen, the best place to survey the entire room, and from that outpost Serena had a clear view of Nate for the first time since the night of Blair's wild graduation party. While Serena had danced her butt off, Nate had sat on the floor, looking more baked than usual, until he'd finally stood up and randomly kissed little Jenny Humphrey. Captain Archibald had been so pissed when Nate failed to actually bring home his diploma that the day after graduation he'd driven Nate off to East Hampton himself, to begin his summer of labor. Serena hadn't had a chance to say good-bye but she'd known she'd see Nate again soon. And here he was, sporting a deep, been-outside-all-day tan that made his already-perfect teeth look whiter and his already-stunning eyes gleam even more green. His chest looked broader, his forearms stronger. Of course Thaddeus Smith had noticed him.

"That's Nate," Serena announced casually.

"Straight Nate?" Thaddeus wanted to know.

Serena shrugged. "He's up for anything," she giggled. "But it looks like he's not alone."

A very tan, very blond girl was clinging to Nate's arm as though he were a life preserver, digging into his bicep with her long, fire-engine-red-manicured nails. Her eyes were wide open and darting around excitedly like she was on drugs.

A distinct possibility.

"Please tell me that's his sister," Thaddeus whispered. "Is she wearing teal eye shadow? Wait till I tell Serge when I get back to the hotel."

Serena studied the new girl. She was indeed wearing blue eye shadow. She was also wearing head-to-toe peach, which was so . . . *peach*. Her hair was blond and vaguely frosty looking—she looked like Stripper Barbie at the beach.

Stripper Beach Barbie? Now that's catchy.

"And where did she get that outfit?" Thaddeus gasped bitchily.

Serena didn't have time to indulge in more catty gossip: Blair was racing toward her, a panicked look on her face that Serena knew all too well.

"Shit," Serena muttered in a low voice.

"Who. The. Fuck. Is. *That*?" Blair hissed angrily, pushing through the gawkers and into the narrow kitchenette.

There was no need for Serena to ask who she was talking about.

"Oh, honey," Thaddeus declared kindly. "She's nothing for *you* to worry about."

"I cannot believe," Blair snapped, "that Nate had the balls to show up tonight with that trash. Where did he pick her up—the mall?"

Well, there are plenty of those on Long Island.

"Sit," Thaddeus ordered, patting the countertop. "Relax."

"Shit!" Blair took his advice and pulled herself up onto the kitchen counter. "I need a drink."

"Just stick with us," Thaddeus suggested, leaping onto the counter himself and draping a protective arm over Blair's bare shoulders.

"I didn't think it was true." Chuck Bass squeezed past Serena to join the threesome in the kitchen. "But I guess seeing is believing, huh, ladies?"

"Hey Chuck," Serena sighed, leaning against the countertop between Thaddeus's widespread legs. The last thing she wanted was for Chuck Bass to get his claws into her gorgeous costar.

"Blair, back stateside!" Chuck cried. "Good to see you." He leaned in and dropped a quick kiss on each of her cheeks.

"Hello, Chuck," Blair replied, receiving his kisses dutifully. "Who's the mystery bitch?" She might as well take advantage of the one good thing about Chuck Bass: he could always be counted on for the scoop, however inaccurate.

"I heard about her but I've never actually met her," Chuck explained proudly. He took a swig from a freshly opened bottle of Dom Perignon. "Oh! Don't look now," he whispered loudly, clearly enjoying the moment, "but I think we're about to meet and greet."

Nate led Tawny through the thicket on the dance floor toward the cluster of familiar faces in the kitchen.

"Hey," Nate shouted over the din. "Serena. Blair." They looked even more gorgeous than he remembered. Like they'd been sprinkled with fairy dust.

"Nate!" Serena lunged forward to give her old friend a warm hug, trying to prevent the moment from being too unbearably awkward.

Too late.

"Hello," Blair seethed, crossing her legs and brandishing her comically long cigarette holder like a weapon. "Can I please have a light, someone?"

Thaddeus Smith produced his silver monogrammed Zippo and lit Blair's cigarette for her. The song faded into

Madonna's "Papa Don't Preach," and some of the ultra-hyper extras jumped into the middle of the dance floor, pretending to sing with imaginary microphones.

"A real gentleman at last." Blair sighed dramatically. "Has anyone seen my date?" *Just wait until Nate saw her French-kissing with Jason. Hah!*

"Blair," Nate stuttered. "You look great. Welcome back." He didn't know what else to say. *He felt like an asshole.*

Blair hopped down from her perch on the countertop, wobbling drunkenly in her pointy black Jimmy Choos as she landed on the cracked tiles of the kitchen floor with a thud. "Yes, thanks." She nodded. "You'll have to excuse me. I'm really in the mood to dance. I just need to find my partner." She strode back into the packed living room.

Serena smiled apologetically at Nate. "I'm Serena, by the way." She offered her hand to the new girl and noticed that she did have pretty almond-shaped blue eyes and adorable freckles on every inch of her skin.

But isn't she always thinking of something nice to say?

"I'm Tawny," the girl said in a thick accent that made it sound like *Tauh-awe-nie.*

"Right, sorry," Nate mumbled. "Serena, this is Tawny."

"And Thaddeus." Serena squeezed the movie star's arm. "This is Nate and Tawny."

Thaddeus jumped down from the countertop and shook hands warmly, first with Nate, then with Tawny. A drunk girl wearing a purple off-the-shoulder American Apparel minidress backed into him accidentally. He gently pushed the dancing girl away from the kitchen.

"It's great to meet you both," he responded charmingly.

He really is *a good actor.*

"Ahem!" Chuck Bass cleared his throat dramatically. "And I'm Chuck."

"Tawny." The girl adjusted the straps on her teeny peach

backpack and offered him her hand before turning back to look at Thaddeus, wide-eyed and practically drooling.

"Enchanted," Chuck cooed, kissing her hand and bowing deeply. "Let's get to know each other, darling. You don't mind, do you, Natie?"

Nate would have told him no, go right ahead, but he was distracted by the sight of Blair, holding hands with some tall banker-type, laughing with her head thrown back. She was introducing him to an older, impeccably dressed short man, and there was something familiar in the excited way she was flirting with both of them that filled Nate with longing.

"Excuse me," Nate stammered. "I have to go."

As he headed for the door, he heard Chuck say, "By the way, you've really got some tan."

Tawny, indeed.

b is an inspiration

"Darling! Dar-*ling*!" Bailey Winter screeched at Blair. "You must—I repeat, *must*—stay with me on the island this summer. You are *perfection*."

They were standing in the bedroom doorway, which was as far away as Blair could get from the kitchen without actually losing sight of it. She tucked her dark, almost shoulder-length hair behind her ears self-conciously. She'd always liked getting a compliment, but what did you say when someone called you perfect?

How about "thank you"?

"I'm starting a new collection. It's called Summer/Winter." Bailey made a motion with his hands that Blair suspected was supposed to convey the seasons but instead looked seizurelike. "And you, my love, are Winter."

Jason placed his big, soothing hand on the nape of her neck. "That's incredible, Blair," he said sweetly.

It *was* incredible, but out of the corner of her eye, she couldn't help but watch Nate, with his glittering green eyes and perfectly worn baby blue Polo, backing away from Serena and Chuck and that townie whore and exiting the party. Where the fuck was he going?

"And Serena is Summer!" Bailey cried, snapping Blair back to attention. He snapped his mirrored aviator sunglasses off his face and stared excitedly into the overhead light.

Blair made eye contact with Serena across the dance floor. Of course, being one of two muses hadn't *exactly* been part of the fantasy, but if she had to share the limelight with anyone, then it should be her best friend.

How generous.

"I'll need you both to live with me, of course. For inspiration, darling! Don't worry—there's plenty of room for visitors in the beach house!" he singsonged, winking at Jason.

Blair watched Nate bump fists with Jeremy Scott Tompkinson from his lacrosse team out in the hallway. She sometimes wondered how much guys really told one another in the locker room. Had he told them all about the first time they'd had sex? What about how he'd done it with Serena? Blair looked down to see that her hands were suddenly clenched in little red fists.

"Well, I'd love to visit." Jason pulled Blair closer. "If she wants me to."

Bailey put his aviators back on and pushed them down the bridge of his nose. "I'll take you if she won't!" He laughed and then clapped his hands together. "Oh, that must *terrify* you! Don't worry, I don't bite. Unless you ask me to!" Bailey squealed in delight.

Blair set a prim smile on her lips. She was having a hard time concentrating on Bailey's staccato voice. He'd called her perfect—she'd heard that.

Of course she had.

But what was this about living with him? Well, that could work. Although she'd just told Jason she'd be staying here, Bailey's palatial town house on Sixty-second and Park would suit her just fine before jetting off to Yale in a couple months. Surely Audrey Hepburn had had some similar set up as a muse? "I have a feeling my mom will be dropping by for 'tea' every afternoon," she offered.

"Will she be on Georgica, too?" Bailey asked, arching his unnaturally high, dark eyebrows even higher. "How wonderful!"

"Georgia?" Blair creased her forehead. Did Bailey always have to be so strange?

"No darling, Georgica. At the beach house? In East Hampton? Where we'll all be?" he explained. "Are you feeling all right, dear?"

Wait, the *Hamptons*? As in, the Hamptons where Nate and that little townie slut were going to be all summer long? Why hadn't he mentioned that before?

Well, he *had*.

"Yes," Blair confirmed, although she was shaking her head no. "I'm fine."

"I'm afraid the guest house is set back on the property and it's a *bit* close to the neighbors, although they're hardly ever there. Perhaps you know them, dear? The Archibalds? Their son seems to be around this summer. About your age. Devilishly handsome?"

Oh, she knew him, all right.

You know what they say: *love thy neighbor!*

threesome on the roof

Dan clambered up the ladder and pushed open the trapdoor to the roof, climbing outside and into the night. The building wasn't high enough to see the East River, but he could smell it, dank and fishy. Still, there was something magical about dusk in New York in the summertime.

He lit a Camel and puffed on it greedily. Through the uneven tar roof he could feel the beat of the bass and hear the dull roar of the crowd. He needed to sit and think things through in solitude. Strolling to the edge of the roof, he peered into the back garden and in the pitch darkness he almost stepped on Bree, seated near the roof's edge in a lotus position, eyes closed, her turquoise gypsy skirt fanned around her.

"Bree, are you okay?"

"Dan," she replied calmly. She opened her eyes and smiled up at him. "You're smoking."

Shit.

He tossed the burning butt into the night. "Sorry," he appologized sheepishly.

"You don't need to apologize," she said in a voice so neutral it was condescending.

Dan took a seat next to her on the roof as darkness descended. The backyard was so dark he could just barely make out the sparse tops of lilac bushes and the burning embers of people's cigarettes. He closed his eyes and tried to pretend they were on top of a mountain in the Pacific Northwest, but even his poet's imagination wasn't quite that strong.

There's no oxygen up here. Not enough for two . . .

"I won't mind if you want to smoke," Bree continued. "I wish you wouldn't, because it's bad for your body and it's bad for the earth, but you're an individual. You can do what you like."

Dan didn't feel like arguing. He shook out another cigarette and lit it. There. He felt better already.

"I'm sorry you had to come up here after me," Bree apologized.

Dan decided not to mention that he hadn't been looking for Bree, just a minute of peace and nicotine.

"Anyway, I thought you'd be downstairs talking to Vanessa. It certainly seems like you two have a lot of things to say to one another."

Dan didn't know how to respond. The truth was, he didn't really believe he and Vanessa were going to be living together for the rest of the summer as . . . friends.

Friends with benefits, maybe?

"I'm not mad or anything," Bree assured him, and she sounded like she meant it. "We've had a nice time together these past few weeks, haven't we?"

"Totally," Dan agreed, nodding. He knew what was coming.

"I've really enjoyed the experience of getting to know you, getting to understand you a little, as a person. That's always a magical journey, don't you think?"

Oh boy.

"Right, right," Dan replied. Her philosophy-of-life mumbo jumbo was getting kind of old. He'd be glad when he didn't have to listen to it anymore.

"And it's okay to be sad when the journey ends," she said. "But our paths are diverging. Your life path has taken you to a big Hollywood party. That's just not something that I understand. My path is leading me elsewhere."

He'd gambled his education and his entire future on a romance with Vanessa, and he was comfortable with that. But he'd gambled his entire future with Vanessa on Bree? What had he been thinking?

Bree stood and stretched, holding her hands high above her head and exhaling deeply. Only her bright white camisole and white-blond hair were visible in the dark, so she looked like she was floating, legless.

"Oh, Dan." She sniffled a little. "It *is* hard to say good-bye, isn't it? I try to remember what my yogi teaches about letting go of things, but it's hard. I mean, I'm still just a student."

Suddenly it didn't seem hard to say good-bye at all.

Dan hugged her weakly because it seemed like the right thing to do, then watched her disappear through the trap door. He was kind of glad that they were breaking up, and he was definitely psyched she was going to leave. He'd learned a lot from her, about nature, about exercise, about spirituality, but he'd reached his breaking point: he just wanted a cigarette, a minute of peace, and then he'd head downstairs and go home with Vanessa—in a just-friends sort of way.

"Bummer," uttered a male voice in the darkness.

Why was it so hard to get a minute alone?

"Who's that?" All Dan could see was a cherry tip and the telltale scent of a joint.

"Sorry, dude." Nate Archibald stepped closer to Dan. "Didn't mean to eavesdrop. I guess you didn't realize I was up here."

"Oh, hey." Dan recognized the preppy stoner guy who'd broken Jenny's heart last fall. Jenny seemed to have gotten over it pretty fast, though, so there were no hard feelings.

"You're taking it pretty well," Nate commented.

"Honestly, man," Dan replied philosophically, "it just

wasn't meant to be. I thought she was someone I was interested in. I mean, I thought I was ready for a change. But you
know what? I was wrong. I think I just fell into the trap of
being excited by the *idea* of someone new, even though we
were totally wrong for each other."

"Really?" Nate coughed. The thing Dan had just described
sounded sort of familiar.

"The thing is," Dan continued, waxing philosophical,
"there's a girl downstairs, and she's the one, man. She's the
one."

Which one?

"I think I know exactly what you mean," Nate added, his
voice an octave higher than normal. "And that chick was right,
too—there are, like, paths, right, and sometimes they just . . .
diverge. Right?"

Whoa.

"I don't know about paths," Dan replied, even though the
whole paths-diverging thing was actually borrowed from
Robert Frost's poem "The Road Less Traveled," which he'd
actually quoted in his graduation speech. "I'm kind of sick of
all this New Age bullshit, to tell you the truth."

"Yeah?" asked Nate. It sounded kind of cool to him.

Of course it did.

n exits stage left

Nate pushed past a couple of girls in full-on shimmy mode and scanned the room. It was so crowded he could barely find a familiar face.

Or maybe he was just too baked.

He hadn't expected to have any kind of epiphany at this dumb Hollywood party. This was supposed to be the summer when he got serious, when he turned his back on parties and pot and chasing girls who were more trouble than they were worth. This was supposed to be the summer he worked hard and used his hands and did some honest, challenging labor and got to know himself and prepared for his career at Yale. Captain Archibald and even Coach Michaels were determined that Nate head off to Yale a different man, a new man, able to handle responsibility. And now, suddenly, Nate felt like he already *was* that new guy.

That was fast.

Something Dan had said really stuck with him: his life was right here, waiting for him, inside this shitty, overcrowded apartment. The girl he was meant to be with was right here, and the only honorable thing to do was to break the news to the girl he *wasn't* meant to be with.

But he couldn't find Tawny's familiar golden mane anywhere: the place was that packed. Nate pushed his way across the dance floor, ignoring the beckoning wave of some short, overly tanned weirdo who was wearing sunglasses even though they were inside. There was no time for small talk: he was a man on a mission.

Nate slipped into the tiny sliver of a kitchen and hopped up onto the countertop. From that vantage, he surveyed the apartment, looking for Tawny. The apartment was completely packed. There were faces he recognized—Isabel and Kati huddled in a corner, whispering to each other as usual; that pale, grim-looking bald girl was talking to some little kids—but for the most part, the room was crowded with strangers

Then there she was: her distinct blond hair was unmistakable. It was full and wavy and fell over her tan freckled shoulders, one of which was bare where her peach-colored top had slipped off. Nate had to admit it was pretty sexy. He saw that she was grinding with Chuck Bass, who'd unzipped his mint-green shirt and was gyrating bare-chested to a dance remix of that Ciara song. Ew.

Nate felt a tug on the leg of his Trovata khakis and looked down to see Serena smiling up at him.

"Whatcha looking for?" she asked, hoisting herself up onto the countertop beside him.

"Hey," Nate said, helping her up. He was grateful for the company of an old friend.

Serena scanned the room and looked in the direction in which Nate was staring intently, watching the almost-obscene display of Chuck and Tawny dancing.

"You know," Serena whispered into Nate's ear. Her breath was sweet and tickled him pleasantly. It was a nice, familiar sensation. "You don't have anything to worry about. Chuck Bass is just a horny, harmless jerk-off, and we love him for it."

"I'm not worried," Nate told her. "It's not like that."

"It's not?" asked Serena. She knew Nate, and she definitely knew better than to believe him when it came to girls. He basically always got it wrong.

She's an actress, remember? She only *plays* stupid.

"I thought it was, but I was wrong," Nate admitted. "Hey, where are they going?" Tawny had taken Chuck by the hand and the two slipped behind a nearby door.

"That's the bathroom," Serena observed.

Double ew.

"Whatever." Nate shrugged. He'd passed the point in his life where he was interested in girls who slipped into the bathroom at parties with guys they barely knew. He didn't care what was going on behind that door right now. Then, on the dance floor, barefoot and beaming, he spotted Blair, firmly in the embrace of a much-taller guy in a conservative gray suit. Their lips met and Nate had to shut his eyes.

"I'm taking off," he muttered. He'd had enough of this party. Nate shot his familiar, disarming, lopsided grin in Serena's direction. Then he hopped off the countertop and disappeared into the crowd.

cue music, roll credits

Serena remained on the counter and pulled out the cigarette she'd wisely tucked behind her left ear. She smoothed out the wrinkles in her "borrowed" black Bailey Winter dress, turned on one of the stove's burners, and bent to light her cigarette in the flame. She took a long drag, turned the stove off, and turned her attention back to the still-pulsating dance floor.

"Where did Nate go?" Blair stormed into the kitchen.

"Who knows?" laughed Serena, helping Blair up onto the counter next to her. She handed Blair her lit Merit Ultra Light and surveyed the scene with a satisfied smile on her perfect lips. "Where's Jason?"

"He's going down to his apartment," Blair explained. "He's got some leftover fried chicken in the fridge and I'm starving."

"You're so lucky," Serena cooed, taking her cigarette back from Blair.

Yeah, Blair's the one with all the luck.

Serena slipped her hand into Blair's. She leaned over and whispered into her friend's ear, which was adorned that evening with one of those famous Bvlgari *B*s, "This summer is going to be amazing."

Blair set her dark head on Serena's shoulder. "I hope the Hamptons is big enough for all of us."

Serena squeezed Blair's knee in response. Blair surveyed the living room. If she blinked, it looked *exactly* like the party scene in *Breakfast at Tiffany's*. She'd dreamed of this moment so many times, she'd lived this moment, in the movie in her head, so many times over that it felt familiar. It felt wonderful.

There were Kati and Isabel, wearing matching black Tocca dresses and trying to hide the fact that they were whispering about Blair and Serena by smiling and waving excitedly. Blair could practically imagine what the two of them were saying about her. There was Chuck Bass, spinning that fluffy, tan blonde around, his bare chest slicked with sweat. Every other person was looking in *their* direction. Was it Serena or was it Blair who had caught their attention? Did it really matter?

Nope.

The DJ—a frantically sweating guy whom Bailey Winter couldn't stop ogling—switched the records, and he must have been reading Blair's mind: the apartment filled with a taut staccato beat, and then a sexy voice sang some very familiar words:

Moon River, wider than a mile . . .
I'll be crossing you in style, someday.
Dream maker, you heartbreaker . . .

"It's me!" Serena cried.

"You sound incredible," Blair told her honestly, clutching Serena's hand.

In the movie inside her head, this was the perfect closing scene. The music was just right, and the crowd was going wild dancing. An adorable guy was preparing a plate of cold fried chicken for her in his downstairs apartment. Even though it was just an unfurnished dump, the apartment felt totally glamorous. Blair was thrilled. This was her place. This was her party. Sure, the movie might be ending, but really, summer was just beginning.

hey people!

Oh. My. God. I didn't think it was possible to have the kind of hangover I am currently suffering through, but then it's my own fault: when am I going to learn not to overdo it on the champagne? Then again, I always have been the life of the party. And what a party! I'm sure those of you who were lucky enough to be in attendance will agree: the second-biggest, bestest blowout of the summer. Looks like someone is shaping up to be the hostess with the mostest, don't you think?

mix and match

Dying to know who went home with whom? I've got the full dossier:

T is indeed a one-man guy. The second the party ended he grabbed the first available cab and sped down to the Mercer, where he met up with his secret sweetie. I hear the two of them spent the next forty-eight hours ensconced in the honeymoon suite.

That fabulous designer, the one who insists on wearing his mirrored Ray-Ban aviators inside at night, lured that dreamboat DJ back to his manse on Park Avenue, no doubt with the promise of a free outfit from his new menswear line. Wonder if the DJ will be spinning vinyl out in the Hamptons for the rest of the summer . . .

S went to bed alone. Will wonders never cease?

D and **V** shared a taxi back to his—um, their place on the Upper West Side, but the romance is officially dead. Separate bedrooms, people. Separate bedrooms.

N was spotted on a very late-night LIRR train out to the island, all alone. So what became of . . .

Trashy bottled-tan-and-bottle-blond girl? She and **C** kept the party going, hitting the club circuit and ending up at Bungalow 8 at 5 a.m. They still haven't been heard from.

Want to know why **S** went to bed alone? Because her roomie was crashed out downstairs. But **B** was definitely not alone. . . .

if we took a holiday . . .

People, let's not forget that the summer was made for relaxing. July is just around the corner, and by the time Bastille Day rolls around (isn't that someone's birthday?) we'll officially be halfway through the break. There will be plenty of time for work come fall, for midterms and fraternity mixers and worrying about interviewing for the best internships for next summer. This is our time to play, so get down to business and just . . . chill. Oh, who am I kidding? In this town, we never just chill! Okay, maybe N does, but the rest of us never slow down. Speaking of never slowing down . . .

Will **B** break another heart? She's already cast aside two suitors, and it's not even July!

Will **S** be able to adjust to life without the cameras rolling? Will she share the limelight with **B** in the Hamptons, or will she go Hollywood and spend the rest of her days with her new BFF **T**?

Will **N** make nice with **B**? Will he go crawling back to **S**? Or has he finally given up on chasing girls and decided to grow up? And have we heard the last from his little summer fling?

Methinks not. After all, he still has lots of work to do on his lax coach's house. . . .

What about the Hamptons? Will this vacation playland for the rich and famous be big enough for **B**, **S**, and **N**? What about the rest of Manhattan's elite? The location might be changing, but the stars are character actors—they never really change.

And seriously: what the hell is going on with **V** and **D**? Odds are three-to-one they re–hook up by July Fourth. Any gamblers out there?

I'm going to stay on the case and get some answers. It is, after all, my summer job, and I'm the hardest worker I know. Someone's got to do it.

You know you love me.

gossip girl